Biding My Time

Biding My Time

Sarah L Roth

Biding My Time is dedicated to my first reader and fan, my mom. Mom, I'm sorry you didn't get to see the story published.

I hope you are proud wherever you are.

PROLOGUE

10 Years ago…

The glare from the light hitting the mirror was blinding. I stared at the clothes on Sally's bed. The choice of my clothing left little to be desired. The burlap sack in green. The burlap sack in black. Oh, wait my personal favorite the burlap sack in a hideous pattern. I looked like a middle-aged woman shopping at Lane Bryant, instead of a sixteen-year-old shopping at American Eagle.

This party was not my idea of a good time. I've never been popular. Why was I invited? It was Sally's birthday and all the cool people were attending. I scanned the board over Sally's desk and compared myself to the pictures. There was one with her other friends. I looked at it and then back to myself in the mirror. They made me feel out of place. Nevertheless, Sally was my friend and a popular girl.

Sally was flawless with her long hair, the perfect shade of chestnut. We were both the same height but she was a fan of heels. Her style was never in question. She made everything she wore look runway-ready. "It doesn't matter where it comes from as long as you look and feel good in it," she would to tell me.

This frizz ball on top of my head was way too curly for anything. My hair was set up in a presentable mess. Luckily my face looked amazing when it was painted an inch thick. I snorted at the thought. Glancing from side to side, my cheeks turned red. I couldn't get over that I looked amazing. Talking to people who normally tormented me, well, that's a whole other story.

"So, who's going to be there?" I couldn't look into Sally's eyes. I nervously picked the nail polish on my already bitten nails.

Sally was way too cheery. "You know, the usual." She looks at me with worry. "Serena, don't be nervous. They're just people, and outside of school, totally different. And I know for a fact Conner will be here." She gave me a wink.

"Conner, really?" I looked down and picked off an invisible piece of lint off of my shirt. "I don't want to see him. You see how he treats me." This had to be some cruel joke.

Conner was my main tormentor and one big crush. He's so beautiful, I can't even stare into his malachite-green eyes. He was built like an athlete. He excelled at every sport. He touted baseball as his one true love or something. I would sit out of sight and watch him play. He had five inches over me. As large as I was, I felt small and insecure next to him.

I huffed and blew a strand of loose hair out of my face. "He HATES me. Besides, he goes for girls that look like... I don't know…. you. Never me." I don't know why it mattered so much to me. Conner always went for the girls who should grace the cover of Playboy magazine.

Her arm wrapped around my shoulder. "Don't start. You're not having this pity party of one. You have so much more to offer. You're amazing. Wicked Smart. You're talented beyond belief." She continued to tick off a list. "You sing, dance, and act. Me? I can't act my way out of a paper bag. Now enough with this pep talk. I'm ready to party."

The party was the one thing she waited for all year. She loved to celebrate her birthday. I have missed her past birthday parties in fear of being bullied. She always wanted everyone to get along. I inched down the stairs, after Sally, (which creaked under my weight) and helped set up. I made her favorite punch and set out the rest of the food.

"I got plans for you," she shouted. "I am going to help you meet someone. You're too wonderful to be spending your weekends home studying. You should be out with me and my flavor of the month." She winked. "You know the pool hall, movies..."

A couple of hours later, the party was well underway. I sat myself in a corner and basically became invisible. I thought I was getting away with it when I heard Sally's voice.

"Everyone grabs a spot on the floor. It's time for truth or dare." She grabbed my hand. I gave her a grave stare and reluctantly moved to the center of the room. I pulled my shirt down in an attempt to cover my stomach and tried gracefully to sit on the ground in the circle.

"Ok, birthday girl goes first," shouted Tiffany. "Sally, truth or dare?"

"Truth"

"You are no fun. Okay tell me, the most embarrassing moment you've had in the last two years."

"That's easy. I had to take drama as an elective." Her face turned into the biggest smile aimed at me. "I had to perform a monologue. I had no idea what a monologue was or how to memorize it. Luckily, I had my girl here to help me." She pointed at me and gave a wink. "I prepared for what seemed like days. I got up on the stage and totally blacked out. Serena was in the same class, and she helped me. She shouted out a line and after my face stopped burning, I was able continue."

"Wow, you're such a goody-goody. I thought you would have said you got drunk at homecoming and threw up in front of Mr. Hall. Alright friend you get to pick the next one."

"I guess I'll pick Conner. Truth or Dare?"

Conner shouted with laughter. "Dare."

"Let me see. No parents here, so... I dare you to go into this closet with my friend Serena." She smirked. "For seven minutes in heaven."

She looked at me like the devil, and I froze. My face felt hot. I gave Sally an evil glare.

He shrugged, "Bring it on."

I had no idea what I was going to do. Do I protest? Do I walk out? Or do I just give in and pray nothing will get back around school? I walked into the closet and he followed behind. I quickly smell my wrist. I'm so glad I actually smelled good. I've been experimenting with new smells and been nervous I would smell like a salad and not flowers.

"You have seven minutes starting now."

What are we, like twelve?

I've never kissed a guy, and a cute one at that. Only in my dreams. Here I am following on a dare that wasn't even mine.

I whispered in fear. "We don't have to do this. We can just sit here in silence for seven minutes." I started to sniffle, trying to keep it together. Stuttering, "I won't…I won't say anything and you can continue to torture me." It felt closed off. It smelled musty and stagnant.

"Serena, I'm sorry." He gently placed his lips onto mine and a small moan escaped. Was it mine, or his?

I felt the air escape me. I let go and gave in. He ran his fingers through my hair and I didn't know how to respond. Why was he sorry?

He separated from me. "Wow! Um... I... How have you never been kissed before?" He stammered.

"No. That was my first," my voice was shaky. A tear came down my face. "Please don't tell anyone." He smiled. I could see the smile through the dark. He reached for me again and we fell to the ground. I never thought he felt that way.

Seven wonderful but painstaking minutes later they all came back, smiling at us. I am sure this was going to be all over school. "Gosh Conner, did that suck? I mean look at her, she's a cow. I would have to place a paper bag over her head," Brian said jovially.

Conner looked at me and mouthed, "I'm sorry." I couldn't take the shaming anymore; I ran up the stairs and cried. I hid on the landing. I had to escape. I was so embarrassed. I felt as though the whole room was closing in on me. How could she do this to me? What was she trying to accomplish?

I could hear Sally shouting at the crowd, "You are all just mean. You fuckers. What did she ever do to you? She is a nice person and you are just evil to her. I was hoping you would see what I see. Maybe if you would get to know her you just might like her too. Look! Party's over! Thanks a lot." I heard footsteps approaching. I quickly ran into her room. I hear Sally running up after me. I slam the door and wait in her room.

"Why? Why me? I like being invisible. Ok, so I am tormented, but for the most part I am invisible."

Attempting to change the subject, Sally asked, "What was it like? Is he a good kisser?" My eyes were welling up and the tears came. "Why are you crying? This was an experience you needed. That you have always wanted." I looked up smiling through the tears. She approached me carefully. "Everyone is leaving and we will spend the rest of the night watching movies and eating cake."

"Sure. Just leave me alone. I need a minute. I need to calm down." Sally left the room. Tears continued streaming down my face because of the embarrassment of what I just participated in. I sat on her bed and just took deep breaths. There was a knock and the door opened. "Look, Sally, I told you I need a minute. I just can't face anyone." There he was, Conner. "I don't want to see you right now. All you are going to do is just use this against me. Get out, Conner. I want no part of you and your harsh tongue. He reached for my face and wiped my tears. I was stunned.

"Serena, do you know why I went along with what everyone says about you?" He took a deep breath. "I did it because..." He took a deep breath and continued, "I don't know. Or I guess don't know who you are."

I looked at him stunned. "Are you drunk? Wait this is some kind of practical joke. Is everyone waiting behind that door? Don't bother, Conner. You don't have to continue; the jig is up."

"There is something about you that is drawing me to you. Your beauty shines from within. I never realized that till now." He continued. "Can you please give me a chance? To talk? To get to know you better?" Caressing my cheek, he looked into my eyes. He continued, "I think I deserve this chance." He kissed me again. It was just as sweet as it was before. Tender and delicious.

I opened my heart for the first time, and fell.

Chapter 1

Serena

Why do dressing rooms have the harshest lighting? Doesn't the store owner want the perfect lighting when a woman is trying to score the perfect dress for their tenth-year class reunion? I swivel my body from left to right attempting to catch a glimpse of my ass in this dress. I'm still not sure. I slouch, looking at the image I see before me. Who am I kidding? I have no clue what I'm doing. This is nothing like me. I'm not normally showy when it comes to my body. The old me still stares back at me, no matter which mirror I pass. The three-hundred pound one. Not this woman who wears a size ten and can wear mostly anything she wants.

An idea pops in my head. I grab my phone and snap a picture of myself in the mirror. The front and then back view. If anyone can tell me the truth, it's my best friend, Sally. Perfect.

"Sal is this, ok?" I type out and click the send button. The air conditioning kicks on and a breeze from the vent above my changing room blows my stray hairs around while I wait. This is the fifth store I have been too in two months. Tomorrow is the night and I want to look perfect.

I mentally hum the Jeopardy theme song in my head. Another three minutes pass. No answer. I send a second text.

"Sal? I feel like my body is too exposed. Tell me the truth." The look I'm going for is utter fabulous. This reunion is happening whether I'm ready or not.

I prop my hand on my hip and pretend the woman in the mirror is anyone other than me. Yes. I see it. Her. Me. The image looking back at me smiles. This is what my friend Sally is always talking about. I am a completely different person. At least on the outside. And this dress will knock him off his feet.

An annoying beep goes off and I stare at the message. "Bitch, I'm not sure. Buy the damn dress and bring it with you."

I'm betting most of my classmates won't recognize me. The new and improved Serena Ashby has arrived. This process didn't happen overnight, but life has changed dramatically since graduation. The old Serena walked right out the door and never looked back. I had one focus, and it was to make myself whole again. I took the time to take care of me. Having accomplished my goal weight, the outer beauty finally reflects my inner self.

Exuding confidence is a wonder in itself. Not only have I lost the weight, my career is better than anyone would expect. I have achieved success as a voiceover artist for the cartoon *Scruffy the Dog*. Even so, I have been itching for a new direction in my career. It's my time to branch out and shine. With some hard work and a little practice, theater auditions in the Big Apple could be the future. My future.

My smile brightens at the cool, confident reflection in the mirror. Swishing the full skirt left, and then right, I decide the dress is perfect. The little black dress is a show stopper with a plunging neckline in front and a back so low I will come dangerously close to showing my butt crack if I make the wrong move. The gold chains draping across my spine gives a dramatic effect. It screams sexy, but not in the how-much-do-you-charge-for-the-hour kind of way.

The fact that he could be at the reunion hasn't been far from my thoughts. My sights are set on none other than Conner Fortenberry. I imagine his jaw dropping in a state of utter shock when the beautiful brunette standing before him is revealed to be his "dirty little secret."

There is a soft knock on the door as a bubbly voice flows through the cramp space. "Excuse me, how is the dress working out?"

I quickly remove the frock and place it back on the hanger. A grin forms as I walk out of the small room with dress in hand. I reply to the sales clerk, "I'll take it." This dress screams Yowza. All I need now are perfect shoes to match.

Everyone who is anyone is going to the reunion. Jaws will drop when they are surprised by my new look. Especially Conner. He won't know what hit him.

My thoughts drift to Conner for the umpteenth time today.

That night, so many years ago at Sally's party, changed me. A single kiss knocked me off my axis. My inexperienced self was shocked when we went further than I'd ever thought possible. He was not only my first kiss, but my first time at running "the bases" — my first everything. The aftermath of that relationship led me here. Conner had said he liked me, loved me even, that he really wanted to be around me. But, of course, it couldn't be. Not really. Not the way I wanted. Not the way that meant anyone else knowing he was dating me.

Popularity controlled the hierarchy of high school —keeping up appearances and all that. And I didn't have it.

There was one thing I could control back then, and it helped shut out the negative. My career path always gleamed in the forefront. Refusing to be a doormat for a selfish, teenage boy and his buddies, I took my dreams by the hand, and now I'm successful. And as I walk past a mirrored wall, I can see I'm not too shabby to look at either.

I spend all day primping, fussing with my hair, and purchasing new makeup to be perfect. Chances are good that I'll run into someone from my past from the moment I board the plane so I want to be ready. A swell of excitement runs through my core at the idea that I'll finally have a chance to tell my tormentors to suck it. I was told in the past to let it go, that we all have grown up and moved on from that point of our lives. I say, Hell No! The pain never leaves. The nightmares never leave. The little voice that questions your worth never leaves.

Racing home to finish packing and arriving at the airport on time is my major focus. I cram everything I need for this weekend in one suitcase. It's a miracle. With the weather so unpredictable, the need to pack a variety of clothes is paramount. It's only for a few days but I'm needing a diverse wardrobe.

My heart races at the thought of being of discovered. I want all my hard work to mean something; especially where Conner is concerned. I want his jaw to drop, his eyes to bulge, his breath to catch in his throat. I want to be the only thing he sees.

When the car I ordered arrives in front of my building, I walk out, rolling out my pretty pink suitcase behind me. I clutch the matching carry-on in the crook of my arm. I take a last look back at the front door of the apartment adorned with gold filigree. My home. My sanctuary.

Here goes nothing.

Deep breath…

And everything.

Traffic in Charlotte is horrendous. From the moment the driver pulled into the steady stream of traffic, I knew the commute would be hairy. My leg bounces on the floorboard as time ticks by. Please, don't let me be late for my flight. I send an oath into the universe vowing not to be a total bitch as long as I make it to my gate on time.

The car pulls up to departures and I throw open the door. The driver grabs my suitcase from the trunk in a single smooth motion and smiles as payment happens before exiting a cab.

My heels are muted as I jog across the lobby pulling the ticket from my carry-on as I proceed to the security line. The painstaking task of removing my items from my carry-on bag adds to my anxiety. After passing through the checkpoint unscathed, I check the screen. Well, all the rushing was for naught since there is an hour delay. I gaze up, shake my head in disbelief at the ceiling, and head to my gate.

I quickly move down the hallway until I see salvation. The oasis ahead of me on the way to the gate.

A bar in my path with neon lights screams 'stop and have a drink.' I pay for a lemon drop shot for liquid courage. Am I really doing this? Well... bottoms up. I raise my glass to no one and gulp it down.

The time is slipping away. I leave a generous tip and head across the corridor at the sound of an attendant announcing my flights boarding order.

The gangway leads to a set of stairs. My brow furrows as I see a tiny tin can of an aircraft before me. Normally I am not claustrophobic, but these types of planes terrify me. I take my seat and stop myself from automatically asking the flight attendant for a seat belt extender. It still astounds me how far I've really come.

In my seat, I sink into the weathered pleathered seat and view my world from the tiny window. I reach into my carry on and grab my e reader to pick up on where I left off with the book I am currently reading.

The flight rushes by. I didn't want to drive back home for a change. Staying at the hotel was a better fit than staying with my parents. My mother asking too many questions that I don't want to answer about my personal life is something I'm not comfortable with.

Besides, I'm a grown adult and if I want to drink and have "fun" I will. I've got plans. Those plans don't involve my childhood bedroom or morning coffee with my dad.

Once we land and deplane, I follow the crowd toward the exits. My eyes scan for a sign with my name. I spot an adorable old man across the baggage claim area with a placard in hand Ms. Ashby. I find my colorful suitcase among the rotating luggage of grays and blacks, and snag it by the handle.

With a smile, I make my way to my driver. He takes my bags and I follow him to the waiting town car. He places my suitcase and carryon in the trunk while I slide into the back seat.

Sounds can be heard of the trunk closing and the opening of the driver side door. The car shifts as the driver is seated inside.

"Ms. Ashby, I have your hotel listed as the Hilton on Crabtree Lane. Is that correct?"

I meet his kind eyes in the rearview mirror and smile. "Yes sir."

The hotel isn't far and we pull up in no time. The driver places the car in park and pops the trunk open. I exit the vehicle and my bag is already waiting for me. This guy is good. I decide a generous tip is in order.

With my Pepto Bismol pink case rolling behind me, I step into the rotating doors and make my way into the large atrium of the hotel. I glance around and spot a beautiful waterfall feature and glass elevators. My brain is on high alert at the possibility of running into someone from the lowest time in my life. I calm myself with a deep breath and exhale. This is my moment. My time to shine. A moment decade in the making. And still, I scan the immediate area for any familiar faces.

The lobby is fresh and inviting with shades of green and complimentary earthy tones. Comfy couches and tables surround a fireplace just begging for me to grab a glass of wine and snuggle into their maroon velvet cushions. Guests lounge around reading, chatting, and clicking away on laptops. You can't miss the entrance of the bar from the clinking of glasses and loud conversations on the far side of the lobby. Music and chatter spill into the large space from every corner and echo off the high ceiling.

A quick perusal proved the coast was clear, so I meander over to the check- in desk. The long row of brown, white marble countertops hiding the computers continue the motif. The front desk clerks stand waiting with their fake smiles on for the guest before them.

When I was younger this would intimidate me. The worry I would turn away and immediately someone would be saying something about me. Now, I remind myself I have nothing to worry about.

Checking me in is a slender brunette dressed in a suit style uniform, synonymous with the brand, I glance over at her name tag, Chrissy. She brushes a lock of hair over her shoulder, gives me a pleasant smile, and searches for my reservation. The clicking of the keyboard fails to echo in the large lobby. After taking my credit card and ID for my verification, she continues to hunt and peck in a rhythm through to my reservation.

"Ms. Ashby, just to confirm you are here for three nights in our junior suite at the reunion rate. You're all set." She passes my key across the smooth marble top and adds, "Oh, I should also mention the bar is hosting a karaoke night this evening, if you are interested."

A smile creeps over my face. Then right on queue she continued.

"I will have the bellman assist you with your bags." She gestured to an older, distinguished gentleman in a bellman uniform. Bar and karaoke. Two words I'm grateful to hear, since singing has calmed my nerves in the past, and built my confidence when I had none.

I follow the bellman to the elevator. My thoughts wander to Conner. I remember a time when he watched me in rehearsal for the school play. He had hid in the back row, but I had known he was there. I had felt his presence.

Wondering if he has arrived yet, I hold the bellman at the elevator and circle back to the desk. "Excuse me? One more thing. Can you tell me if Conner Fortenberry has checked in yet?"

"Of course, Ms. Ashby." A bright smile curled her lips and reached her eyes as she tapped the keyboard. "Mr. Fortenberry has, indeed, checked in. Would you like me to contact him for you?"

I ponder for a moment and glance at the clock on the wall. "No, thank you. I would like to keep my arrival… a surprise. He has no idea I'm here." I flash a smile, and she winks in acknowledgement. She gets my drift.

I make my way back to the elevator bank and rejoin the bellman. The gentleman holds the elevator open for me and starts small talk about the hotel. He mentions he has worked for the hotel for fifteen years. "You know your voice sounds familiar. Where have I heard you?"

"Have you seen Scruffy the Dog? I play the voice of the grandma and Scruffy's friend Rosie?" The elevator made the climb to the tenth floor. Each number changed my heart would smack against my chest a little faster.

"Yes! My grandkids love that show." His voice has a lilt. "They watch it all the time. Wait till I tell them who I met. You will be more popular then when

I met the President." The doors open and I follow the bellman to the left towards my room.

He opens the door and hands me back the key. The bellmen walks through the suite giving me a quick tour. As I walk into my home for the next few days, I gasp at the size of the suite. I pull out some bills kindly tip the gentlemen and thank him for his help.

Once I shut the door I sit on the sofa. It's very comfortable and inviting. I glance around the room again, and with a chuckle, I whisper to myself, "Membership definitely has its privileges."

With so much to do I decided to let the unpacking begin. I pad across from the couch to the room where my luggage resides. I lay my suitcase on the bed and the metallic zing of the zipper echoes in the spacious room. I remove my toiletries, stashing them in the bathroom for easy access. Little bottles of shampoo, conditioner, soap and lotion await my smell of approval. They will have to wait. My is focused on the reunion dress from the store. I pull it out, still in its protective covering, and hang the little black number on the closet door.

After I busy myself putting all of my clothes and toiletries in their designated spots, I decide to take a moment time to relax and pick up my e reader. My schedule with the show rarely gives me time to do anything. After forty-five minutes of peace and solitude, restlessness takes over. I get this feeling of ADD. My eyes do a once over of the room, I wish Sally was already here with me, filling the space with her firecracker personality. I try to find comfort in the fact my best friend will be here tomorrow glamming me up for the main event. Until then I need to find some way to amuse myself, and there is only so much one can do in a hotel room alone.

The reunion is tomorrow, and I'm going stir-crazy overthinking things. Exhaling a huff, I push myself off the bed, check my hair, and apply a light touch-up of my makeup. With hours… minutes… seconds ticking by to the event, I need a form of release.

As if in a trance, I grab my hotel key and head for the elevator. I press the key for the lobby. Waiting and watching for the numbers to descend down. The elevator stops on the fourth floor and a cute older couple gets on. He is holding her hand and kissing it. Looking into her eyes like she is the only one there. I wish for something like that one day.

The elevator makes the final stop to the lobby and we all exit.

I cross the hotel lobby and enter the bar. A cool breeze wafts across my neck sending my senses onto high alert as I scan the smoke- filled room and spot a familiar man accepting a drink from the bartender. There he is— the one who's plagued my thoughts for years. I saunter up to the stool beside him. He looks up, searches my face and, just as I expected, doesn't recognize me. I gesture to the empty spot. "Is anyone sitting here?"

"No," he replies and extends a hand. "I'm Conner." He is dressed in a pair of dark colored jeans and a button-down dress shirt. My gaze immediately falls down to his empty left hand; no ring, not even the hint an imprint. He's as handsome as ever. My Conner hasn't really changed, the only noticeable difference is his curly hair is now shorter and tamer. The rusted-nail hue of his curls always did compliment his striking emerald eyes.

Think Serena. Think... I draw a blank. What do I say? Do I come right out and say who I am? I'm not ready to see the glimmer in his eyes disappear. In a stroke of sheer genius, I extend my hand. "I'm Lila."

"Nice to meet you, Lila. What brings you to Stoney Woods?" He clasps my hand and shakes but his eyes narrow as he studies my face.

"Relocating." I stutter, not anticipating this question. "For my job," I add. "I was living on the west coast, and my company decided would be an asset on the east coast accounts. Or maybe they wanted to see if I can tough out the winters."

He laughs and my heart flutters. He always said I had a good sense of humor. But, I have to remember I'm not Serena right now, I'm Lila.

Narrowing his eyes with a hint apprehension he says, "Your voice sounds familiar. Have we met before?"

"I don't think so." And with that, I move my attention from him and look for the song binder. Without looking back at him, I move toward the make-shift stage and thumb through the pages. I mentally thank the hotel for having a fun night all planned out.

I select a song and saunter back to the bar as if I had never has never walked out on our conversation. With a finger in the air, I move to the signal the bartender, but Conner blocks his line of sight.

"Can I buy you a drink?" He touches my arm and send electric sparks along my nerve endings before motioning to the bartender himself.

I stiffen and hesitate. Deer in headlights is the most appropriate description of the emotion racing through me. Finally, I yank my hand away. I don't know if I can continue this charade. Maybe I should just get it over with and tell him. I begin to speak, but my mouth refuses to form the words. Instead, I nod at his offer.

"Sure. Cosmopolitan. I know it sounds cliché, but I love them." I tap my fingers on the bar to the beat of the current song. "I love my vodka." The phrase rushes out of my voice as I trip over my words. My nerves send a flood of heat that redden my cheeks.

"So? Karaoke, huh?" He nods toward the stage. "You could never get me in front of people to sing."

"It's fun." I nudged my shoulder against his. The fluttering renews. My eyes lock on his, searching for some kind of acknowledgement that he has the same reaction. If he doesn't feel it, I'm setting myself up for disaster. "You should try it sometime."

"What are you going to sing?"

"An old favorite," I answer as the MC shuffles the request papers around mindlessly in a fishbowl. He plucks a slip from the bowl and holds it up to what little light is there to get the right song queued up.

A devious smile spreads across my lips as I reach for the drink the bartender places in front of me. Liquid courage takes the edge off my anxiety. I lift the glass and sip the concoction, the taste of lime and cranberry tangoing across my taste buds.

The MC shouts, "And now, let's bring to the stage... Lila."

I stroll up to the stage. My sapphire blue top fits my curves snuggly and skims the top of my favorite

21

pair of jeans. I add an extra sway to my stride to let my midriff peek out. A sexy pair of Jimmy Choo shoes, that- elongate my legs like there's no tomorrow. round off the look. I have watched way too many episodes of Sex and the City, and read way too many issues of Vogue, to not know how to throw a killer outfit together.

I grab the microphone as the title appears on the screen. With a deep breath, I let the intro play. The words start their slow ascend on the screen, but I don't need them. I knew them by heart. "How do you cool your lips, after a summer's kiss?" rolls of my tongue. A look of recognition crosses Conner's face. His expression says sure your voice sounds familiar, but the song... The song is a dead giveaway, and yet, I couldn't help myself. He probably deserves it.

Controlling a stage is a special quality few possess. Fortunately, I've dedicated my entire career to learning such skill, and for the rest of the song, I own the stage, catching every high and low note with pinpoint precision. When I wrap my mouth around the last word, the bar patrons erupt into a synchronized raucous of claps and whistles.

I bow to the crowd as Conner's gaze meets mine. Exiting the stage, I make my way back to my seat. Something unsettling hits my gut when I notice Conner's frown.

"I know I asked this before," he shakes a finger at me, "but are you sure we haven't met? From the sound of your voice, I would swear you sound exactly like…" His eyes narrow as if a ridiculous thought crosses his mind. "Nah, you couldn't be her."

"Who?" I feign egging him on.

"Someone from high school." He sighs, then takes a sip of the amber liquid in his glass. The burn of the alcohol reddens his cheeks. He's still handsome.

He must realize he's staring at me because he quickly changes his demeanor, tearing his gaze away from me. "Someone who I hurt. No, shattered. Someone who didn't deserve it and makes me wish I could fucking take it back every day."

I peer at him over the top of my martini glass. "Sounds like you weren't always a very good guy." I watch as my words land.

When the bartender checks our end of the bar, Conner motions for another drink, and his glass is filled with whiskey once again. He downs it in one gulp. "I'm here to, hopefully, fix the shit I caused all those years ago."

I glance at him and sip my beverage.

We sit there for a while, talking about our jobs. Over the years, he'd worked hard at acquiring his degree in finance, then his MBA. Now, he's involved in banking. Stocks, mortgages, managing? I have no idea. My mind blanked out and all I could do is stare into his eyes when he speaks.

Managing a bank is something I couldn't handle. All that money and responsibility in my hands would be dangerous.

Conner asks about what I do. I was extremely proud of my job, so I explain the ins and outs of being a voice for a cartoon. He is a better listener than I was. He hangs on every word, seeming impressed with me. When we talk about relationships, he says he isn't married and has no kids, which means he likely hadn't seen the show I am currently working on.

After reacquainting ourselves with one another, and another drink each, I am pleasantly numb and at ease. In an attempt to flirt, I wrap my hand around his arm, occasionally squeezing his large bicep as we talk. When an opportunity arises, I plant a quick kiss on his cheek.

There is a break in the karaoke programming and the music changes. We look at each other and the unspoken energy crackles between us.

Conner rises to his feet and offers his hand. His eyes beg me to take it, and I want nothing more than to do it. My hand fits in his like they were made for one another. He leads me to the dancefloor where he guides my hands around his neck before encircling my waist with his. We start a languid rock to the music, seemingly comfortable in each other's arms. Dancing with him makes me wonder what my prom would have been like, had I gone.

His eyes burn into mine. Those beautiful green eyes with specks of gold. They send shivers down my spine, straight to my core.

Just as I feel myself slipping into their depths, it happens. In the breadth of a second, he presses his lips to mine and kisses me; and, boy, do I remember his kiss. Memories of how he felt against me, and how our mouths melded together, come rushing back. It's the kind of kiss that makes one weak in the knees. I always forgot where and who I was—and now, for the life of me, I can't remember why I kept my identity a secret.

He pulls his lips from mine and grins. Oh, yes, he felt it too. "Do you wanna come up to my room?" My breath is ragged and my heart races.

Lacing his fingers with mine he gestures, "Lead the way."

As I head to the elevator, I think now would be a good time to tell him the truth. Maybe he would still want to be with me even if he knew who I was.

The elevator doors open and our reflections meet one another. The slow burn in his eyes moves up and down my body in the mirrored wall before he glances back at me. He gestures for me to enter first and walks in right behind me. The doors slide close. The spacious elevator shrinks as the realization hits. We are alone. Utterly alone.

I flick my top back forth to cool me down. The closer he stands the hotter I get. He gives me a smoldering crooked grin, and his demeanor changes. With that one expression, he melts all the icy walls I've worked so hard to build, stomping on the resolve I've struggled to find. Powerless. I am absolutely powerless.

Conner presses the fire button and elevator jolts to a stop. Memories of Seven Minutes in Heaven flash through me. "I know who you are..." He corners me to the back-right corner and my face flames with heat. "The game is over Serena. You can't fool me for one second."

Oh, I'm fucked. Game over. He reaches over, presses the button and we ascend to my floor.

His fingers brush a fallen tendril of hair from my face as he leans in, pressing his lips to mine.

I inhale through my nose, suddenly breathless from our connection, and kiss him back one more time.

The car climbs floor by floor. I turn back to the doors and refuse to look back. My gaze focuses on the numbers. It feels like hours while I watch them until ten illuminates on the panel.

Chapter 2

Serena

We link fingers and step off the elevator. The hallway stretches before us, leading to my room. Placing the key in the slot and removing it quickly doesn't work. It keeps showing red. I check the number on the envelope and match it to my key just to be sure. My frustration gets the better of me and I start to laugh. Conner chuckles and I feel like a dumb ass.

"I'm sorry about this. You would think with all the travel I do, I would able to get the key entry on my first try."

Next thing I know, he takes the key from my hand and, slips it in and back out with ease. "I believe you need to take it slow. Slow and easy does the trick." He winks at me and holds the door open.

I pull away, trying not to get sucked under the tide of emotions rolling over me. I smile and clear my throat. "Do you want to come in?"

He stares deeply into my eyes and steps away. "I think this is where we say goodnight."

"Goodnight?" He can't be serious. "You can't be serious. I thought maybe we would get reacquainted?" I move closer and place my hand on his cheek and kiss him again.

He squints at me suspiciously, then nods. "Serena, we have all weekend. This isn't over."

I glance over my shoulder at him as I step inside. He smiles and retraces his steps down the hallway to the elevator.

Once I see him walk away, assured he is not returning, I walk into my room. I toe off my shoes and sit on the sofa. My feet throbbing from heels is nothing new but rubbing my own feet didn't quell the feelings. The kiss in the elevator plays over in my mind and all I keep remembering is the time when we were stuck in the closet.

Rising from the couch, it feels like an inferno rages in my clothes and now they seem way more constricting than they were earlier—or maybe my body is more sensitive in his company.

Walking into the bedroom, I closed the door behind me and panic.

I glance at the clothes in the drawer and find my pajama pants and a comfy tank top. I strip out of my outfit and replace it with my pjs. Placing my hair on top of my head in a messy ponytail, I return to the lounge area.

Swinging my feet onto the cushions, I tuck my knees to my chest and hug them like a blanket hiding my insecurities. My bare feet lay on the couch exposing my polished toes.

As my sobs begin the phone rings, and I hiccup a startled gasp. The only person who knows of my whereabouts is Sally. "Hey Sal. What's going on?" I try to hide the sadness in my voice as much as possible.

I fall back onto the couch and slip into a mute trance.

Her happy, high-pitched squeal radiates through the earpiece.

I pull the receiver away from my ear and grimace.

"What's going on? I'm so excited about tomorrow!"

I roll my eyes and place the phone back against my ear. "You just saw me last week. Yes, it was on Skype, but hey, you saw me." I chuckle then release a big huff. "I saw him, Sal. He was in the hotel bar."

"Did he recognize you?"

"No, not at first. And I led him to believe I was someone else, too. I think he had suspicions, and then we got into the elevator... He stalked me to a corner and knew it was me. Conner locked us in the elevator and kissed me till I was week in the knees." I took a gulp of a breath holding back the tears.

"Sally he wouldn't come in. He said we have all weekend." I started to cry.

"Serena, you are a beautiful person. You have every right to have these feelings. The only question is, do you still care for him?"

"I don't know. Right now, I need to show him, them, that I am better. That their harsh tongues- and the endless bullying I endured, can't hurt me anymore." I sniffle, emotionally drained from the night, and then change the subject. "I gotta run and get some sleep if I want to take Zumba in the morning."

"Okay. I'm done chatting with you anyway. This bitch needs her beauty sleep!"

Later, as I pull back the covers, I think about how much I'm looking forward to the dance class in the morning and letting off some steam. I climb in the bed, schedule my wake-up call, and nestle in for some much-needed sleep.

Chapter 3

Conner

How could she think I didn't know it was her? How could Serena think I wouldn't know her anywhere? Her eyes were always so damn captivating. I see them every night when I close my eyes. Hell, she's the dream I most often dream. That crazy woman has been tempting me from afar for the last ten years and I will do whatever it takes to win her back. Every girl I dated, kissed, slept with, they never compared to her. She is always in my head, taunting me.

I head down the hallway toward the elevator and press the button. Once the doors open, I choose to head to the lobby instead of my room. Leaning back against the rail, I scrutinize my reflection in the elevator doors. I scratch the scruff on my cheek and shake my head disapprovingly at the sorry sack of shit glaring back at me. Did the words *this isn't over* come out of my mouth? I sound like a crazy ex. Was I even an ex? It's not like anyone knew we had ever dated. Damn it! I really need a drink.

My whole goal in high school was to be popular. How shallow was I? My parents thrived on success, and I wanted to make them happy. Appearances meant everything to them. They would never understand what I saw in Serena. All they would've seen was a fat girl who was beneath me. I hate that she was the one good thing that's ever happened to me and I had to hide my true feelings for the sake of what they wanted.

Serena paid the price. She always paid the price. Every time I said a hurtful word, did a harmful act, or supported the wrong side. I fucked up. I leaned on her for support, and treated her like garbage. And yet, that gracious girl let me return to her time and time again.

Memories keep haunting me. The Monday quarterback in me keeps replaying and trying different scenarios. How could I have kept all the balls in the air? Maybe I needed this ten-year journey to evolve and grow, into a man deserving of her.

Now full circle, and I intend on proving my love is true, no matter what the past held.

Exiting the elevator, I walk toward the hotel bar, only I wish I wasn't alone. Since the day I lost her, all I feel is alone. Sure, I tried getting her out of my system, but it never worked. She lurked in my thoughts giving me a disapproving glare with every woman I dated.

I approach the bar, and the bartender, seemingly aware of my frazzled demeanor, pours me a shot and slides it toward an empty stool before I'm even seated. I shoot the whiskey down, slouch on the stool, then order a beer to chase it with. The server pops the cap off and passes it. I need to figure out how to win her back.

My thoughts swirl in a hazy blur of liquor to that kiss. The one at Sally's house. The one that made my head and my heart go to war with each other. The one that made me yearn for a girl who I wasn't supposed to want. The one that still had me wanting her even all these years later

Looking back on it, I understand the ramifications of my actions, but then it seemed important to be popular and successful. And as much as I should point the blame to my superficial and shallow parents' example, I had to own my own part in the hurt I'd caused the beautiful person that just sent me packing once again. My heart faltered. Coming this weekend had been a step towards making amends for being such a prick to Serena.

Back then, when we were alone at her house, her ease, smiling without a care in the world, drove me crazy. Witnessing Serena with her guard down was the best fucking thing in the world.

I didn't know I had the power to change things. I could have kept my popularity and still been with her. I believed no one would accept the change— accept us.

I scour my hand over my face and take another sip. The lingering warmth of the whiskey causes the beer to scorch as it glides down my throat. I suck in a mouthful of air to cool the burn.

That damn song. Why did she choose that song? It brought back memories. I guess any song she sang would do that to me. She always could get to me when she sang. Her voice is like an angel's.

My cell phone buzzes against the sticky bar. I glance down at the blurry text message on the screen. Holy fuck! Sally.

Sally: Boy oh boy, did this turn to shit!

Me: I have no idea what you are talking about.

My phone blasts the absurd tone I selected for her to make sure I pick it up. I obediently answer, "Yes, Sally."

"Don't you, 'yes, Sally,' me! I warned you, she wasn't ready."

"I didn't start shit. She hit on me saying she was someone else. Like some twisted…" I caught myself. "She lied to me, but I'm not a fool. I played along." I rubbed my tired eyes with my fingers. "Fuck, I missed her."

"Look, she won't admit it, but she's missed your sorry ass, too. You're going to have to jump through hoops to make sure you don't screw this up again. *Capisce?* I will try to help on my end. Be prepared, though, she's not the same girl you remember. She is not as soft-hearted as she once was. You broke her. It's been ten years, and we all know you are the one that took her down. She hasn't trusted people the same way since."

Sally hung up leaving me feeling worse off than I did before. What did she mean? How did I break Serena?

Chapter 4

Serena

Ten Years ago

"Serena? Serena? SERENA?" My mom shouted. "You have a visitor. Wake up. You've been asleep for a couple of hours. Napping in the middle of the day? Teenagers," she shook her head as I bolted upright in bed. "Conner is here."

I knew she wasn't thrilled. His name fell from her lips with disdain. Mom knew I craved friendship and acceptance. But she could only see the down-side of my friendships.

"Why you hang out with him, I don't know. Hasn't he done enough damage?"

"He's a nice guy," I grumbled, rolling my eyes. "I know our circumstances are strange, but we have fun hanging out."

"You're right. I don't understand it, but the first sign of trouble, he's gone."

I climbed out of bed and headed down the hallway, stopping in the bathroom to do a quick once-over. After brushing my hair into a ponytail, I padded to the living room.

Conner was sitting on the couch petting my dog. Frodo, the ever-perfect lap dog, didn't even know I was there. The pup rolled on his back demanding for a good belly rub. I glance down and see Conner's hand scratching as Frodo moved his hind leg up and down in excitement. Once my gaze met his, he stood.

"Hey, I was in the neighborhood and was wondering if you were free to maybe hang out?"

Of course, I was. I was free almost every day because I didn't have such a huge social calendar. "Maybe. I was thinking of calling Sally and seeing what was going on since... I don't know... she's never afraid to be seen with me."

"I'm sorry, but you know I can't. How would it look?" He sarcastically waved into the ether. 'Hello, have you met my girl, Serena?'" He leaned me back and kissed me. "'Yeah, I torment her, but, what the hell, she likes to play the victim.'" Conner took a step back and looked directly at me. "Suddenly, we're together after I treat you like shit at school? Look, this conversation is not how I wanted to spend my time with you. I was hoping we could watch tv, or play cards, or something." He lifted his eyebrows in a suggestive motion. I pushed past him toward the door in the hallway.

"Well, I was going to do some dusting in the basement. How are you with a rag and cleaning supplies?"

"Good. I'm good. I've never seen the basement before."

"Great," I drawled sarcastically, smiling as big as possible. "You're in for a surprise. Hold on a second." I lift my face toward the ceiling and shout so my mom could hear me. "Mom, we're going down to the basement to dust Grampa's stuff."

A muffled voice reached back, "Okay."

We descended the stairs and turned left. I stopped, placing my hands on my hips, and grinned with pride. There it was—Grampa's old bar. It was like saying 'hi' to him every time I saw it. I missed him living close. The home we lived in first belonged to my grandfather. He did a lot of socializing and decided building his own lounge in the basement was a fun refuge.

When he moved away, this became my hangout. I often sat on my throne- the single red barstool in the middle- and did my homework. On the other side of the bar was his shuffleboard table. It was one of my favorite games to play. On the opposite end of the shuffleboard table squatted a couch and a coffee table. A green-felted bumper table sat in the massive open space behind the couch.

Conner's wide gaze scanned over the basement then landed on me. I smirked at his astonishment as I flipped on more lights and clicked the knob on the radio. A Def Leppard song played, and I sang along, dusting the glasses behind the bar.

I paused and gave him a stern look. "Thought you were helping me." A smile crept over his face. "Well, if you are, come on then." I tossed a dust rag at him which he caught before it hit to the floor.

He joined me behind the bar, his lips pursing in that sexy way they did when he wass trying to look upset when he really wasn't. "Why haven't I seen this before?"

"This is where I hide out from everyone to be alone with my thoughts. Maybe do my homework or jam out to some music. I don't share this place because everyone would want to hang out here. Only Sally knows." I winked. After a little cleaning, we moved to the shuffleboard table. I wiped off the board, but Conner seemed uninterested in playing.

He grabbed my hand and led me to the couch. My face warmed and suddenly I was embarrassed, scared, I don't know. An uncontrollable sigh of frustration betrayed my emotions. The hurt I was trying so hard to hide. "What do you want, Conner? Why even bother?"

"I just want to talk. I know I'm an asshole." He grabbed his hair in frustration. "My whole life I had to be perfect—wear the right clothes, have the right friends. Hell, even my activities were picked out for me. But, you... you are... something I picked out on my own." He sits me down and brushes a hand down my cheek. His eyes changed; they were softer. He picked up my hand and kissed the back of it. Something was different in him. Maybe, he was different.

Chapter 5

Serena

The phone wakes me with a start. What the… Ugh, the wakeup call. I want to shout, "Two more minutes, Mom.'" Instead, I get up, walk to the bathroom, and ready myself. If I am going to be staying in the area this weekend, I am going to take the class.

Since my transformation, I have grown accustomed to working out. It's an obsession of mine. I freak out if I miss too many days in a row.

The clerk last night was kind enough to point me in the direction of the local chain gym. I had checked online and saw they had an early Zumba class, and I'm ready to get my body pumping. The endorphins will clear my thoughts.

After a quick Uber trip to the studio, I walk in and find a place in the lineup. The instructor is a young woman with boundless energy. I follow her every move as she bounces around at the front of the room, shaking her perfectly toned ass in front of the mirrored wall, and screaming instructions into a headset. How in the hell is she so perky for this early in the morning?

I slouch over, exhausted from my mind running over last night's events and the hyperactive instructor directing the class. Glancing at the wall of mirrors to my right, I realize my hair is unruly and stuck to my face. I take the hair tie from around my wrist and secure it on top of my head in a tight pony tail. Staring my instructor down, I weigh the option of ducking out early and giving into my sleepy state. After a moment of consideration, I decide, fuck it. If she can do it, so can I. I skip back into step with the rest of the gasping woman and finish the class strong. Coffee is in my future.

I head back to the hotel room and call my mom to finally check in. She's always concerned when I travel alone. She has no idea I'm in town, but thinks I'm nowhere near home. I'm sure she can figure it out. She can sniff out my whereabouts like a bloodhound.

I have been dreading this call. Mom answers on the first ring, like she always does. "I know you are not home. I called your landline, then I called the front desk of your building. A very nice man informed me he saw you get into a car with a couple of bags yesterday. So where are you my dear? Let me guess you did come to the reunion."

My muteness on the other end speaks volumes and before she says another word, I blurt out, "Mom, Sally will be here in about two hours. Don't worry, I won't be alone for long."

Mom curses under her breath, "Serena, tell me you are going to stay away from him." My silence tells her otherwise. "Have you seen him?" she asks in a more cautious tone. After another beat of silence, answers her own question. "You saw him already, didn't you?"

Yes, and he is still handsome. "Yes, Mom, I saw him, and he's very happy to see me."

"Sure, he is. Don't forget how I found you that day. How we had to pick up the pieces from his behavior."

A knock at my door saves. I open the door to find Conner, standing on the other side of the threshold looking like the devil in those dark-washed fitted jeans. He doesn't play fair. To rush the end of the conversation, I push for a close with her and gesture for Conner to enter. "Mom, I gotta go. Someone's at the door. I think it's the room service I ordered." Conner's head whips back, and he smiles at me, amused, and I wink at him.

"Okay dear, just remember what I said." My eyes automatically roll. Here we go again. "I don't want to see your heart broken again. Ok?"

"Yeah, Mom." Will she ever stop? "I hear ya. I'll talk to you later. Love you! Bye!" I hang up the phone.

"So, I'm room service now, huh?" Conner walks over, all smiles.

"I can't let my mom know you're here, in my room. She would flip. Again."

"Serena, how old are you? Are we seventeen again and in your basement? On your couch?" He inches toward me and tucks a loose lock of my hair behind my ear. He wiggles his brows, and I chuckle. "Afraid of being caught? We're adults now. I think you're alright." He moves in closer. Suddenly, all the air escapes my lungs and warmth is spreads from the tips of my toes to the top of my head; my whole body is on fire from his nearness.

I come around, inhaling deeply, and push him away. "Yes, we are adults," I say to him adamantly, "but my mom was there during the fallout."

Conner frowns in confusion at first. The disappointment washes over his face, regret clear in his eyes.

"Conner, it's all in the past. I've moved on and had a pretty good time doing it. I'm not the same wallflower who was in awe of you. We can be friends, but anything else...," I shrug, letting my words trail off.

"Friends, huh? Do friends kiss each other like this?" He cups his hands on my face. I stare into those granny smith-colored eyes. He moves a whisper away from me. His gaze scans over my expression with a profound recognition. Though I look different than he must remember, his smile says he knows me, the real me- no matter what I look like. He places a gentle kiss on my lips, stealing my breath. He can still work me. All the teenage lust and angst, the possibility of a future, and the familiarity of an entwined past nearly bowls me over with a single kiss.

"I guess friends can kiss like that," I whisper dazed. What the hell is wrong with me? I stop myself. "Wait! No! What are you trying to do to me? There you go again, confusing me. I worked you out of my system like the demon you are, and here you are bringing back the damage. You need to go."

He stops me mid- sentence. "Give me a chance. I've changed. I am not afraid of being with you anymore."

Chapter 6

Serena

Pushing down the memory of our first kiss, I shake my head at Conner. "First of all, I was asking you to leave so I can get a shower. Sally will be here in an hour." He struts forward, following me as I attempt to distance myself, but I stop, place a hand on his chest waiting for him to realize my intent, and gently push him back. "Secondly, how do I know you aren't afraid to be with me because I look like this and not the person you bullied with your friends?"

"I guess you will need to wait and see." He walks back toward the door. "Won't you?" Conner opens the door, flashes a grin that makes me weak in the knees, and leaves.

After a moment of staring at the door in frustration over Conner's confidence, I rush for the bathroom. I need to be ready to hit the town for shopping with Sally. An earlier text saying she forgot something she needed for the reunion still baffles me. Her mind must be elsewhere too, because she's always been the most organized friend I have.

We've both been looking forward to this weekend. She wants everyone to see the new me just as much as I do. The bullying had been relentless back in the day. I would walk home from school, and the kids threw rocks and shards of glass at me. It would take hours for Sally and me to pull the rocks from my hair. We were disgusted. I was embarrassed and all I wanted to do was crawl in hole and die. That's what they all wished I would do anyway.

My least favorite form of torture was the time I sat at my desk and someone had arranged tacks on my seat to see if they could make me pop. The name-calling was particularly cruel too. They called me Shamu, an elephant, fat lard, you name it. I was nicknamed it at some point.

I never knew who my friends were. Classmates would be friendly to my face, and, in the next minute, turn on me and tell my secrets to the highest bidder.

Despite all of that, I always trusted Sal. Sally and I have known each other since junior high, and I knew she would never betray me. I trusted her, even though she ran with the popular crowd. How she could be my friend and still maintain their friendship was beyond me. And she certainly tried to mix me into her other social circle. Sally tried to include me in her parties, trips to the movies, and the occasional mall visit. Her friends treated me like I was a terminal disease. Or as if Sally pitied me.

"Can you come over and help me pick out what to wear. I have a date with James, and I am kinda nervous. He makes me nervous in a good way. I have no idea what I am going to wear. Help," she screamed.

"Okay, okay. I will be over in fifteen minutes."

I place my hand over the phone and shout out to my mom, "Running over to Sally's be back in a little while."

I whisper to her. "I will be there soon." I hang up and stuff my feet in my sneakers.

I reach for the door and face my mom. "I'm taking my bike so I won't be out too long." I brush past her and her disapproving stare as I slam the screen door and run around back to my bike.

Three blocks later, I greet Sally's mom and head up to Sal's room. She's standing in front of her mirror, with her head tilted to one side, in deep concentration. I looked at her puzzled. How can one boy drive her absolutely bonkers?

She holds up two different shirts, finally noticing I was there. "Should I try this one," she asks, thrusting out a blue short sleeved polo, "or should I wear this one." She drops the blue one and flings up a purple button-down. She keeps switching them in front of her, one then the other. At the same time, she shifts from one foot to the other, showing only the coordinating shoe for each shirt.

My gaze turns to her face. Comparing the differences between us makes my smile turn downward. Her beautiful auburn hair is so straight and long. I am very envious of her. Where Sal's hairs looked sleek and fashionable, no matter how she wore it, mine was an unruly mess of tight curls I must wrangle into a dull-brown ponytail every day. Her eyes are a vibrant violet where my brown eyes are obscured by glasses too large for my face with thick coke-bottle lenses. Luckily, I only have to wear them sparingly. I am fortunate that my mom heard my cries and thought contacts were an innovative idea. I need them if I want to work on the stage. Fogged lenses in the middle of a big scene are not fun.

"Sally, either shirt is fine, or you can go with this green one right here." I held up an emerald green top with a V-neck that is tailored to hug all her curves in just the right spots.

I'm going through a foreign indie movie phase, addicted to Circle of Friends. Who could not love Chris O'Donnell and Minnie Driver? Bernie Hogan, she was brilliant, or so Jack said. The term always stuck with me, and I thought, if I used the words I learned from these movies, it would make me appear sophisticated and cool to the popular. "With the jeans you have on and this shirt, you'll look brilliant."

"Serena, I know you are trying to make 'brilliant' a catchword here but let's save it for Europe."

The sound of someone entering Sal's room catches my attention, so I glance over my shoulder. Tiffany saunters into the bedroom with her chin held high and not a strand out of place. She is my perfect nightmare. She never accepts imperfection. How she and Sally are friends I had no clue. Sally is my friend, so she could've been guilty by association, yet she stood tall against these idiots.

Tiffany stops just inside the door and looked from Sally to me. The moment her eyes met mine, I started to mentally hide. "Who is using lame terminology?" She blew on her nails, feigning disinterest. "Oh, it's you Serena," continues to look at me with disgust on her face. Like a dog ready for an attack.

"Tiff, lay off of Serena. She was here helping me pick out my outfit." Sally continued pulling shirts off hangers and pulling them over her head before yanking them off to try yet a different one. "Which one?" she whines, turning to Tiffany for help.

Looking at this scene, I'm done. I pull my shoes on and started for the door. "Sal, I think I am going to go."

Tiffany peers through the mirror her searing gaze boring into me through the reflection. The hint of satisfaction in her smirk shakes me to the core. She's gotten what she wants. She's torn me down with minimal effort and made me feel unwelcome in my best friend's house. "Good, Serena. We don't need your fat ass taking up space." Tiffany spun on her heels and grinned from ear to ear. "Besides, me and Sal should get ready together anyway. Conner asked me out, and our guys decided to make it a double-date."

I am absolutely mortified. Sally's wide eyes and gaping jaw tells me she didn't know. The sharp sting of jealousy stabs through the pit in my stomach, and all I can do is remain silent. I bite the inside of my cheek, pretending Tiffany's comment made no difference to me. Hell, even if I did tell her about Conner and me, it's not like she'd believe me. "Why do you hate me so much? What did I ever do to you?"

"You exist." She blew on her nails, yet again, and rolled her eyes. "You breathe. You are not one of us, so stop trying to be like one of us."

"You know Tiffany maybe she doesn't need to be 'one of us'? Maybe she is perfect just the way she is." Sally interjects on my behalf.

"Perfect? She is nowhere near as perfect as us. Remember where we come from Sally. We get the guys." She points to her chest "We get the clothes." She points again. We get everything."

With that remark, I don't even respond. I just murmur a goodbye to Sally and bolt before the tears stream down my face. In the distance, I hear Sally trying to stop me. I didn't want to be anywhere near that place. I needed to seclude myself away from this and maybe set up a plan for myself. I was stupid to think Conner would want me not as his dirty little secret. How dumb was I?

Chapter 7

Serena

I hear the hotel door fly open and bang against the doorstop.

"Never fear, I'm here!" Sally rushes in and stretches her arms out for a hug.

We decided sharing a room for the reunion would keep us, meaning me, out of trouble. I say it's a good call, if last night was any indication. My mind relaxes now that she's here.

Sal wheels in her in her giant suitcase, and I chuckle at the amount of clothes she's brought. She always packs heavy, but this seems extreme even though we made plans to stay a few days after the reunion for our own mini-vacation. We'll party at some bars, get in some spa time... the fun, girlie shit.

I run to her. In my mind, we look like one of those corny slow-motion movie scenes where long-lost friends meet for the first time in years and skip toward one another in a meadow full of flowers and chirping birds, then break into song and dance. "Sal!" We hug for what seems like an eternity. The long moment causes me to hold her out at arm's length. "I am so glad you're here. As you know, Conner is here, and guess who has been up my ass since he figured out it was me? I don't know if I should be flattered or annoyed that he likes me now."

"Just wait until tonight, when all eyes are on you. What did you used to say?" She taps her index finger on her chin, staring at the ceiling as if trying to recall something. "You will be brilliant. You will knock them dead."

My cheeks heat from embarrassment and I laugh. Oh my gosh, that was such an awkward phase for me.

"Sal, you remember. Of all the things I used to say, you remember my Euro catch phrase stint." I chuckle and then quote my favorite lines Bernie speaks to Jack at the end of the dance.

"Serena, if there is one thing you are not, now or have you ever been, a rhino."

"Sal it's a line from Circle of Friends, remember? You know, Bernie finally gets her dance with Jack. That's where they started to fall for each other."

"Oh yeah. Well, I always thought Conner was your Jack."

"Was he?" Was Conner my Jack? I consider it for a moment. "I don't think he was ever meant to be mine." My mouth pulls taut. "What did I ever see in him? I mean, I was his dirty little secret for so long, and why? Because I was a person whose size meant something to him. He cared for me when we were alone, but the minute people were around, I was a nobody. A pee-on." Tears sting my eyes, as I begin to cry. "So, maybe this story is not supposed to have a happy ending."

Sally places her hands on each of my shoulders and gently squeezes, offering comfort. "I know I am the only one who knew what went on between you two, but I was there when you left. And I was there giving him updates on what you were doing. He never stopped wondering or asking about you. I honestly don't think he's seriously dated or cared for anyone the way he did for you. I think you need to see if he can make up all the hurt. Give him a break." She points to the fabric hanging from my door. "By the way, you need a new dress. That thing screams funeral, not party. Now look, I need to get my shop on, so come, peach. Don't make me call our best gay for the mission."

"Charlie is here?" I smile, thinking how happy I am to have someone besides Sally to dance with.

"OMG! Yes! He's here. He was checking in when I arrived."

"Alright then, let's run out now, so we can see him later. I grab my purse and run out the room. I'm excited to see what we can find.

At Macy's, we search through every rack and case in the store. Sitting pretty, on a display tower of their own, we find the sexiest shoes ever. And instead of the dress I had planned to wear, Sally convinces me that a short red number would be great with the strappy gold heels. And, of course, with the new assemble, I have to make a pit-stop in the lingerie department to buy matching underwear, since my current situation won't do.

I'm confident that, with my new ensemble, I will be able to make any straight, available guy at the reunion fall to their knees.

We find a little café and sit down to grab a quick bite to eat. During these moments with Sally, I realize how happy I am so happy to have my friend here. We are more like sisters than friends. I just wish we lived closer together. She made her life down south in Florida, and I lead a life near here, doing what I love.

"So, I have some news I think you'll be thrilled over."

I stop my forkful of salad midair, halfway to my mouth, and wait for Sally to continue.

"I'm moving back. My company has decided they want to open an office in Charlotte and they want me to head it."

I let out a squeal, barely able to contain my excitement. "That is the best news ever. When are they wanting you to move to Charlotte? I still have the spare bedroom. You can totally stay with me. You could be my roommate actually. That would be beyond amazing."

She looks so seriously at me, and then her frown turns into a smile. "Sally, I'm not that messy. I'll pick up after myself… I promise…"

She tries to fake sadness in front of me. Nice try but... Um… NO. "Of course, I will. How could I turn down an opportunity to room with my best friend? I am super excited."

"As long as we don't have to re-live the time you introduced me to porn."

Sally chuckles. "Look, I thought it would be a good idea to raid my father's videos. Who would have thought it would give you nightmares of men cuming all over your face."

"I know, we were bored. There were only so many episodes of Jersey Shore one can watch, or rice krispy treats to mess up because we didn't have enough butter." Those were the best times.

"Hey, the Situation is still cute." She grabs the bags and inspects them making sure we didn't forget anything. Looking back to me she continues her comment. "Hot actually."

I blush. "Yes. Yes, that is true." I glance at my watch. "Ok, let's get back to the hotel and start getting ready. As you are aware, I will need help taming this hair of mine." Shopping has caused my smooth curls from earlier to coil out in frizzy fringe around my face. At least they are the right shade. It took me years to get the desired color of red on these locks.

Chapter 8

Serena

We arrive back at the hotel and start the ritual of getting ready. Shower, change, hair, makeup. Done.

We have a bottle of wine, along with some goodies, delivered, to the room. We're ready, like Romy and Michelle. Ready to rock this reunion.

Though I liked the black dress I initially bought for the event, I am so glad Sally talked me into shopping for a hotter number. I am going in style, from my red dress that is tight in the waist and flows out to a full skirt, right down to the sexy, gold heels and the red lipstick. I look like one of those nineteen forties pinup models. My hair is pulled tight into a bun not a strand out of place. I decided on an updo to showcase my smokin' hot dress. I must say Sally is right I look hot.

I chug my glass of wine to calm the nerves that are synchronize swimming in my stomach. There is no time to eat before we should get downstairs for the party. I'm scared as hell. In a sheer moment of panic, I forget what I'm doing here.

Sally sees the fear bubbling and hands me another glass of wine. "Quick. Drink this. We need to leave before you change your mind."

"I can't do this." I gargle through the glass. "This was a big mistake. You go without me. I'll hang here and order room service."

With one swift movement I'm passed my purse and pushed out of the door. The words Hell No! roar at me from Sal's perfectly lined pink lips.

We enter the ballroom and check in with the two ladies posted by the door. They have name tags complete with our senior year photo. Wow has times have changed.

We walk a little further, and there are pictures blown up from the yearbook. The sports teams, clubs, and my personal favorite, the senior musical. I had prepared for weeks to audition. I studied the music, watched the movie. And...

I proved to myself and my class that I knew where I belonged. Not many can say they handled their audition with the script behind their back. Not that I was showing off. Well, maybe I was showing off a little. I worked hard and trained my voice daily as my instrument and my classmates deserved to see that I was driven and had a purpose. I have no time for their games anymore. My goal was to get into a good college and ace my auditions. And I did. Looking at the picture now gave me the courage I needed to venture farther into the ballroom.

"Serena, oh my goodness, it's you." A shrill voice sends the hairs on the back of my neck to attention. "I didn't recognize you. It was the picture on your name tag that gave it away." I look at the woman with no idea who she is. Then, I glance at her name tag and gasp. It was her. One of the many I couldn't forget- Susanne. Susanne was the worst of them all. The crank calls. The awful names. She even showed up at my home once with some people wanting to beat me up. I never knew the reason why. Susanne moves closer to give me a hug like I was a long-lost best friend.

I glare at her coldly and muster the courage to speak. "Well, if it isn't one of the people who ruined my high school existence. I didn't recognize you either." I plaster on a fake smile. Wanting to say so much, but reeling in my hatred. After all this is a happy occasion. "But, I guess, it's because you don't look the same, either."

She gasps. Her tone changes to one of regret. "I'm sorry. I was wrong. We all were. Some people won't admit it, but I will."

"You made my life hell. The things you said and did. But, thank you, I needed to hear it. I was lucky the turmoil you guys caused gave me the drive to succeed." I see someone approaching me out of the corner of my eye. I sigh. Conner. "If you'll excuse me." I prepare to make a mad dash for the other side of the room until he shouts my name. It's too late.

"You look great, even better than last night."

I turn around as he strolls toward me, back straight, chest out, and looking so good he was the only one in the room who could capture my attention with a smile. He kisses me on the cheek and my face heats from the interaction. Why does it feel the whole room has turn to stare at us?

I smirk. "Don't you think you should keep your distance from me. You don't want to start new rumors, do you?" I try to walk away, but his tight grip on my elbow brings me to a halt.

"Come on, Serena. Please. Give me a chance."

I pat Conner on the shoulder. "Dear." Pat. "Old." Pat. "Friend." Pat. Playing hard to get. "I am not sure that a chance with you will be worth it for me."

He winks at me, and I am completely dumbfounded. I never want to hurt again like he hurt me. I don't want to relieve the pain of the rumors after our time together, how I cried and closed myself off from the world, and how trusting another man was a concept so foreign, I never even tried having a serious relationship with anyone. I take a deep breath and sigh. "I can be friends, but there is nothing else I want from you. We will never happen," I promise. After a brief pause, I gather my resolve and push aside the animosity. If we're going to be friend, I need to be pleasant. "So where are you living these days?"

Conner hesitates for a moment, letting my words sink in, then he nods and answers, "Actually just a few towns over from Charlotte. Where are you residing? I take it you aren't relocating."

"No way, I live near here too." I chuckle. I can't tell him that I'm glad he lives close by. He will try to break through the tiny crack in my heart. I offer him a polite smile and step around him, feeling the heat of his gaze on my back as walk away. "Well, if you'll excuse me, I see someone I would like to say hello to."

Chapter 9

Conner

I search every face in the crowd for Serena. She is all I really care about. I wish she could see I've changed. I don't care what anyone says. I spot her, across the room, beckoning me like a siren in a red dress. Oh, that dress. It is unreal how excited I get just from seeing her. My body vibrates with a desire to be close to her. The shoes are out of this world, transforming her legs into sexy as sin limbs. All I can think about is how they will look wrapped around me.

Get those thoughts out of your head. You are here to make amends and win her back. And, I will win her back. I can't begin to explain my true feelings for her.

"Oh shit-nuggets, Conner. Who's the hottie at the party? She doesn't look like she went to school with us." Gary drapes his arm over my shoulder, drooling. "She's gonna be in my bed later, man."

I can't take it anymore. I reach up, wrench his hand into an awkward position, and twist as he tugs it off my shoulders.

"Ouch! Why are you being so rough?" Teasing he adds. "You know I don't like that domineering shit." He shakes the pain out of his hand. Still trying to get my attention… "You know I don't like being topped from the bottom…" He taps on my forehead. "Conner… Conner… Earth to Conner."

I see red. "You will not be having her." I'm seething. Looking directly into his eyes, I growl, "She is mine."

"Who is she?"

I give him a look. The look.

"NO WAY!! That cannot be Serena. I totally didn't recognize her." Gary's eyes roam over Serena from head to toe. He whistles and raises his eyebrows, "Wow time and some weight loss did her good."

I grit my teeth.

"I guess we won't need to place thumbtacks on her chair to see her pop tonight either." He chuckles, and I ball my fists at my sides, barely able to keep my knuckles from smashing into his pointed nose. "Come on, Conner, I'm only being funny. Give me a break. Or maybe she'll give you a break—break your bed." He doubles over as if he'd just told the funniest joke ever, and laughs until tears gather in his eyes.

I jerk him up by the collar, and suddenly his sense of humor disappears. His eyes get as big as dinner plates. "Look you need to grow up you asshole. I have listened to your shit and snide comments for far too long. You are like a brother to me, and it would hurt me if you had to breathe through a straw." Gary's gaze drifts to a spot behind me. I turn, forgetting Gary's idiocy, and see Drinkle hitting on my girl.

Drinkle has no idea who he is talking to? Can he not look at a name tag? I overhear him asking who she was with, and can he see her name tag with picture. She appeared to be having fun with this guessing game.

I drop Gary and hurry over to Serena. She jumps as if surprised to see me, but I have no clue why. I need her to realize I am waiting for her. One day, I hope to make her understand it doesn't matter what she looks like – I'll always want her.

"Come on, can't you just tell me who you are? Conner, do you know who this is? I have been racking my brain over it," Drinkle slurs while teetering on unsteady feet.

"I'm not sure." I play along. I caress her shoulder and trace it with my finger. Goose bumps rise all over her flesh. "Whoever you are, I am pleased to meet you." I dip my head next to her cheek in an intimate gesture, ensuring Drinkle knows she's mine, and breathe her in. She smells like honey and vanilla. I want to lick her like an ice cream cone. "Can you show my friend and I your name tag? Pretty please?" She shudders under my touch, grins, and points to her name tag. Drinkle's eyes nearly pop out of his head when he recognizes Serena's high school photo. Now who is laughing?

"Oh, my goodness. Drinkle, do you see who this is?" I wink at Serena, feigning surprise.

His face turns red from embarrassment. "Wow, Serena, I had no idea it was you. Do you want to get together sometime? So we can, um, catch up. See where this could lead?"

Serena's eyes grow wide and then turn to disgust. She reaches up and pats him on the head. Then she shakes her head no. "I don't think so."

Serena turns toward my direction. Her mixed emotions confusing me. She rushes past me with sadness and lust on her face. I didn't know one person can look like that.

I hang my head in shame and give her the distance she needs. All this positive attention she is receiving must be very strange to her. I look around, and it's something straight out of the Twilight Zone.

I continue watching her from afar. Charlie strolls into the room and heads straight for her, embracing her in a tight hug. If he wasn't gay, we would be having words. Fondness in Serena's eyes sparks my jealousy. I want her to look at me that way.

Chapter 10

Serena

"Charlie. Is that you? Oh, my goodness, I heard you were here." I collide with him as soon as we spot one another and squeeze him tight. "Boy, have I missed you. I know we are all on Facebook and email, but it is certainly not the same." My five-five frame is so much shorter next to his six- foot- three frame. I am extremely glad for my great pair of heels.

He looks especially good. He is wearing a dark suit with a gray shirt unbuttoned at the top—likely some new indie designer on their way to fame. It must be nice to work in the fashion industry. Charlie was always amazing with a sewing machine.

"Serena, my friend. It is so good to see you. Your pictures don't do you justice. You look amazing." He points his finger up and down at me. "So, why were you talking to Conner? I know that can't be easy on you. I mean, with what he did to you..." His voice trails off.

"Look, a lot of therapy has gotten me to this moment. I can see past it and try to be friends, but anything else would be hard. It was like Jekyll and Hyde. He was one way with me alone and then in public he was hateful and rude. I tried to be patient and understand why, but in the end I never did."

"Alrighty, I want the number to your therapist if you can analyze that away. I am going to mingle, and, I think, you should do the same. I will catch up with you later." He turns around, spotting one of his old crushes, and wanders off in their direction.

As the party goes on, we dance, we drink, and some of us Drama Club people pose for some pictures and reminisced about the good old days. Before I know it, it is time to go. I say my goodbyes and enter everyone's' contact information into my phone.

Leaving the few people still enjoying the night's event behind, I head toward the elevators. I should've known I wouldn't be alone. As I proceed down the hall, I feel a tap on my shoulder but don't turn around.

"Sally, I thought you said you were going to the bar for a little while to catch up with some other people. I don't need an escort."

"Who says you need an escort," a deep voice asks.

I stop in my tracks, a little surprised to find Conner walk up beside me. I shouldn't be surprised, since he's been watching me all night. I can't shake him. He is now being way too persistent and, as some would say, acting like a teenage girl.

"I didn't get a chance to talk to you, and I need to get some things off my chest."

"Like what, Conner?" I start the whiny play by play. "That you're sorry? That you didn't mean to make me feel inferior? That, maybe, you were wrong for going behind my back and telling people, who I never trusted, what we did back then? That I cried for weeks over it and never fully recovered. You have some nerve to dredge all that up for me. Did you even try to contact me during that time? NO. Stop the broken record. You just want to feel like you are a better person by apologizing." I can't hold back any longer, and the tears streaming down my face. I run toward the elevator to escape before he can follow me in. I'm not so lucky. He sprints after me, slipping past the doors before they close. "What floor?" I huff.

I wait a few seconds and when he doesn't respond I stew in my own thoughts and jab the button for my floor. We ride up in silence, the tension intensifying between us with each ding. The elevator opens, and I step out with Conner trailing me.

I hesitated as I open the door. I don't want him here and yet I can't let him go. I want him near me. The smell of his cologne and whiskey is a heady combination.

After the way I acted downstairs, and the way I feel… I'm not sure what I want to hear from him. I step into my suite, toeing off my shoes, then hurry to the bedroom and change. I need the distance, even for a moment, to get myself in check. Lingering in the bedroom, I yell, "Look, I'm tired. We can do this tomorrow."

"Sure, we can do this tomorrow," Conner says sarcastically. "We both know it won't happen if I leave. You'll find some excuse, and I'll never get the chance to speak. So, I'll wait here all night if I have to. I'm not leaving before I've said my peace," he knocks then clamors through the door. "I'll wait. I'll wait all night, if I have to," he continues, "We need to talk this out now." Knock… Knock… There are some things that are needing to be said. I never let us die in my book. Knock… Knock…You never left my mind. Not one single day."

Wait. What? I shake my head in disbelief. Holy Shit! I open the door. I get ahold of myself and sit on the couch. I sit with my arms crossed. "This better be good."

Chapter 11

Serena

"Serena, I know my stupid actions a long time ago were wrong." He combed his fingers through his hair. "I wish I could take back what happened after that night. I was a coward, and I never meant to hurt you. I was seventeen and naive."

"Would you like to know what I endured after that night?" I move forward, determined to make my case, and jab my finger into his chest. "You made me feel safe and wanted. You made me feel beautiful. I believed in you." I throw my hands up in defeat. "When you told me you believed in us… What a farce that turned out to be." I need some distance. I step away and walk toward the tv where the mini bar is stored. I don't care how much those little bottles of Absolut are I want one. I take my mini bottle of vodka and stomp back over to the couch. After opening the bottle, I get a whiff of the Russian delight and shoot the bottle down. I place the empty bottle on the coffee table, crossing my arms. I struggle to control the anger beginning a slow boil in my blood.

"But you were wanted. I never lied about that." Conner kneels before me and places his hands on my knees, turning me in his direction. Forcing my eyes to look at his sad face. "I never lied about wanting you or being with you. That was the best night of my life. I truly love...," he stops. He takes a deep breath and continues, "I cared for you more than you realize. I still do. I wish I could turn the time back and change things, but I can't."

"Then why did you tell your friends we had slept together when I asked you not to? I begged you afterwards never to say a word to them. I knew they couldn't be trusted. The whole school stared at me and passed comments. The whole school, Conner! I can never forget their snide remarks, especially from Tiffany. That bitch had the audacity to come up to me and asked me if I paid you... or better yet asked if it was a suicide mission. Like I was some ugly creature that didn't deserve anything. Do you know how much damage that did to me? I never trusted anyone again. I stayed home locked away from everyone. If it wasn't for Sally, I would have retreated entirely. She never gave up on me, when all I wanted to do was die from the shame and embarrassment YOU caused me." I got it out. Finally, I said what I held back for so long from him, from me. His eyebrows raise and eyes widen. He is stunned. Hell, I stunned myself. I had no idea the strength exuding from within me. He looks like the bottom dropped out from under him. "Your actions made me regret everything to do with you. How could you think I would pick up with you where we left off after so many years?"

"I never knew what happened. All I knew was your attitude changed." Conner talks fast as if his life depends on it. "You stopped seeing me. You wouldn't take my calls or respond to my notes. Sally told me to give you time. All I wanted to do was be around you." He inches closer and strokes my cheek. "I even came to see you before you left for college. I wrote you, hoping someday you would forgive me. Your mom told me to leave you alone, that I had done enough damage. So, I did." He buries his head in his hands. "I want another chance. I am not that stupid kid. I'm not seventeen and caring about what other people think, when I should have been strong enough for both of us."

"Well, I am strong for me now. I have to be dependent only on myself and no one else. It took me a long time to get here." I turn away and ball my hands into fists, fighting the emotions itching to break free. I steer my look with a steely expression and turn back to face him again. "I don't need you to be strong for me. That girl, with no self-esteem, has disappeared. I can get anyone and do anyone I want. What makes you think I want to get with you?" Cause I really want to. I'm trying my darndest to appear strong on the outside, but on the inside I'm scared, and my walls are crumbling. I can't go down this road again.

I get up and walk to the door. I pause then yank the door open. My curt words rush out in a rapid staccato. "Now, if you'll excuse me, I am going to sleep. I'm done with this conversation."

Chapter 12

Serena

Conner stands and skulks toward the door. Instead of walking out, he pulls me toward him. We're so close, all I can focus on is his parted mouth. I lick my lips in anticipation. He crashes into me, devouring my mouth with the perfect combination of soft and rough. The kiss is incredible. I try to fight it, but I give in.

He steps back, dragging me with him, and nudges the door with his foot. We both flinch from the loud bang as it slams shut. "Sorry, I guess I don't know my own strength," he says between kisses. His tongue delves between my lips, and I swallow his moan. Conner maneuvers me to the couch, and lays me down. "Serena, this is giving me a severe case of Deja vu. Except, this time, we are going to take our time. No rushing or worrying that someone will walk in on us."

I chuckle. "You probably don't know, but I'm sharing a room with Sally?" My breath quickens as he trails kisses down my neck to my shoulder. "She can come back at any t...t... time," I stutter with a gasp. Am I really allowing this to happen? I have tried to fight this for so long. Here he is. Here we go again. "Just cause this is happening, does not mean we are going any further. This is an itch we are scratching." I can't let him in my heart again. He shattered it once, I won't let it happen again.

He starts to peck soft kisses along my neck again, and I lose all sense of self-control. He places his hands on the hem of my top, and with a quick tug, it was over my head. I gasp in shock.

"I waited ten years for this." He gazes at me like I am his last meal. "I had fantasies of what I would do if we ever had the chance again. All I want is to be inside you, to feel you again."

His hand reaches out, caressing my collarbone, as his eyes devour me. He skims his fingertips down my chest using a feather-light touch giving me goosebumps. The pressure and warmth of his palm increases, messaging my right breast while he ducks his head and gently sucks my left nipple into his mouth. I sigh with pleasure.

Suddenly distracted from the waves of lust rolling between us, I hear voices in the hallway. The slide of a key and a turn of handle unlocking the door. We hold our collective breaths and stare at each other, listening intently. Recognizing the laughter outside the room, I exhale and roll my eyes. We have been caught. "Crap, Sally is back."

We scramble to find my shirt as if my mom was about to walk in on us. Conner snags it off the floor and tosses it to me then plops back on the couch next to me like nothing happened. I yank my top over my head and take a deep breath, hoping the heat in my cheeks subside before Sally enters.

After another shrill giggle and a muffled goodbye, Sally pushes the door open. The instant she sees Conner's back to her and me looking at her anxiously, a knowing grin spreads across her face.

What are we teenagers again? I shouldn't be embarrassed. And, I most definitely shouldn't feel sad about the distance between me and Conner right now. My gaze falls to Conner, who looks very amused by my frazzled state, then lifts back to Sally. She wiggles her eyebrows, and I can't help but laugh.

"Hey Sal, your timing is impeccable as always."

"Whatever do you possibly mean," she replies in a tone higher than normal and clutches her nonexistent pearls. Sally rounds the couch and faces Conner, appearing as if he ate the proverbial canary. "Alright Conner, time to go." She scoots him along. What is she? My mother? "You have your own room, and you need to give this poor girl a break." She grabs him by the forearms, forcing him to rise. Conner stands and crosses his arms. She arches an eyebrow and rests a fist on her hip when he doesn't budge any further. "Laying it on rather thick aren't ya?"

He purses his lips defiantly and glares at Sal before focusing his attention on me.

"It's not over, Serena." He gestures back and forth between us. "We WILL see each other again. You can bet on that." Conner leans in and chastely kisses me on the cheek before he exits.

I giggle as Sally shoves the door shut in his face when he turns around and opens his mouth to say something else. Conner grumbles from the other side, "Ouch! Thanks Sal I think you broke my nose."

I have never seen him so twisted in knots before. I have to admit, I find it rather interesting and refreshing.

I compose myself and grab a can of diet soda from the mini-fridge. "Why is it I can't control myself when it comes to him?" I take a sip and allow the liquid to coat my throat. "I really don't need any of this in my life. I need to process these feelings I'm having. Thank goodness you walked in when you did."

"Serena, he's messed up. He has been searching for you for a long time. Conner kept contacting me from time to time to keep tabs."

"What?" Sally confirms it. It's true! He really has been looking for me? Me? How is that possible? I flick my thumb back and forth over the can's pull tab, trying to hone my nervous energy so I can think. "That can't be true. You would have told me"

"It's true. He contacted me, your mom, anyone he could. He hates how things ended. Your mom told him to leave you alone, in not so many pleasant words."

I glance around the room, air escaping from my lungs. I'm perplexed. "She felt like he'd mess you up again, if he stayed in your life. After all the therapy — all the meds — you were finally on your feet again. She did what she thought was best."

"Remind me to thank mom for meddling in my life." How could this happen? I grab onto the end of the couch, my head swimming with confusion and astonishment. "I can't believe her. I really wanted to be happy with him no matter how it was." I fall into the couch and slouch forward. "Or I thought I did. Who knows? If I was never removed, would I have had the courage to change."

Chapter 13

Serena

The reunion threw me off my axis. I didn't realize it would take two weeks to get back to normal. My schedule now never falters; work, an exercise class, and then home. The one thing I have to look forward to is Sally moving in this weekend. Thanks to the reunion, Conner thinks he has an open line to contact me. Of course, he found me through Sally's Facebook page, and, like a wanton idiot, I accepted his friend request. Maybe I was wishing for that request to happen. So, to get his goat going, I'm posting important things I'm doing. Maybe they aren't important, but I want Conner to suffer, thinking I'm having a good time without a mere thought of him. I wish it were that simple, though. All I think about is him. I need to snap out of it. Conner is someone I should never have gotten involved with. He is part of the old me. The three hundred pound me. The dirty little secret me.

Today, my schedule is taken off course by an unexpected phone call from my old college friend, Ivan. Ivan, who has become a professional ballroom dancer, invites me to help him work through some new routines and, maybe, stay for a new class he will be teaching.

I grab my red leather dance bag with the beige ballroom dance shoes and leave my apartment. I decide to walk from my apartment to the dance studio to get the juices flowing.

I quicken my pace with excitement as I approach the doors to the studio. This is a special treat, since I haven't gotten to wear my dancing shoes in quite a while. I feel so free when I dance. Being led helps me clear my thoughts and let go. The beauty of the highs and lows. How everything ebbs and flows. How a certain pattern of steps can create such beauty.

I met Ivan while studying in college. He was a student in the dance department. Lucky him, he comes from a long line of professional dancers. He helped me through the tough times and watched me transition from obese to healthy. At one time I had a crush on him, but he never saw me in any way other than family. Ivan taught me ballroom after the studios emptied for the evening. I was his guinea pig on certain occasions, when he needed to work through a piece without judgement. I did give constructive criticism when asked, though.

Ivan even begged me to attempt an amateur competition. I always laughed, answering, '"Why would someone want to see this heifer on the dance floor?"'

His response was always the same, '"Because you have more grace in your pinky than some of these dancers out here have in their whole body."' Why he is not on Ballroom Blitz yet, I will never know.

I stroll into the studio in my dance attire. I brought both pairs of dance shoes I had for Latin and ballroom, since I have no clue what he wants to work on. Last month, it was a jive, and I thought I was going to die from over-exertion and lack of oxygen with all the bouncing.

Ivan jogs over to me, pulls me into a tight hug, and takes my hand. "Hey, Serena! Ready to work?"

"You know I am."

He smiles, and I'm reminded of how comforting it is to be around him. He's family. I rub my hands together like a mad scientist. "What are we working through tonight?

"Waltz." Ivan clasps his hands together and waits for my reaction.

"A waltz, huh?" I try to contain my delight at first, but my body hums with joy. I grin from ear to ear. I love the waltz. It's so graceful, especially with all the elegant spins and long, statuesque necklines. "What is the song you chose?"

He glances up from his iPod and smiles brightly. His eyes never fail to light up a room when he is happy. "So She Dances."

"I love that song, Ivan. It's the perfect song for the waltz." I walk over to the seat in the corner and set my bag down. "Ok, let me get my shoes on, and I will be ready. "Can we warm up first?" When Ivan nods, I sit in the chair, strap my shoes on, and begin a quick stretch routine.

An hour into rehearsal, Ivan comes clean with a little secret. "I am hoping you will work with me again. I need to videotape this for an audition."

"Audition?"

"Yeah, Ballroom Blitz has come calling." A big smile streaks across his face. He raises his arms as he sashays backwards through the room. Ivan looks as excited as a child on Christmas morning.

"That is wonderful. About time," I squeal. I follow him to the center of the room.

"Well, I don't think anything will happen, but, hey, you never know." He grabs my hand and spins me in circles.

We practice for thirty minutes, letting our bodies do the communicating. Eventually, I get lost in the music.

When Ivan notices my mind is wandering, he says, "You seem a little disconnected, and I am having a hard time leading you. Care to share with the class?"

I blow out a forceful breath and slump out of my dance pose. "Ok. You remember I went to my reunion a couple of weeks back? Remember the history lesson I gave you about Conner and myself? Well, history has come back, and aggressively."

"Oh, no. That asshole?" He stiffens, pulls his hair and starts shouting something in Russian. My face goes blank, not understanding what he's saying. From the sounds of things. they appear to be curse words. When he finally stops, he offers me his hand and says, "Sorry, sometimes the only way I can express anger is in my native tongue."

"Ok. Seems he is sorry and wants to rekindle whatever we had back in high school. I'm not sure whether it's because of me or what I look like now. Other than that, I do have some good news."

Ivan arches an eyebrow in interest, waiting for my response. "Care to share?"

"Of course." My lips curl into a coy smile. "Sally is moving in. She will be here on Saturday."

"Oh really? I am glad to hear it." I see the wheels turning in his head as he mulls over the tidbit of information, I gave him, then he smirks. I do believe he has always had a crush on her but never pursued anything. "I remember your friend. She is really nice with a toughness about her. She was always protective of you. He glances to the side, recalling a memory from some recess of his mind, and chuckles. "She threatened me once or twice when she thought I had an interest in you."

"Puh-lease, back then, I certainly did not look like this." I nudge my chin to my reflection in the mirrored wall. "I never thought you would look my way." I wink at him.

"I am only going to say this once. You and I are friends. Fat, thin whatever. You. You, were always, and still are, a beautiful person. Never, ever forget that."

I start to tear up from the complement. I never take compliments well because I never knew if they were genuine or not. Ivan has said nice things to me in the past, but for some reason, today, it finally hits me. "Ok. So, let's run this section one more time and call it a night. Don't worry, Ivan, Sally will be here this weekend, and I will make sure she comes with me next time." I give him a devious Grinch- like grin and step up, assuming our dancing pose.

Ivan's cheeks redden slightly as he nods his head. He lets the subject go, avoiding any more teasing or scheming from my end, and creates his lead frame to my following frame. I giggle and, soon, we are whisking around the floor in a waltz. I fall into the magic and freedom of dancing with Ivan for the next hour.

After Ivan and I finish practicing the routine three more times — without a hitch, I might add — I am beat. I go home and slug through my nightly bedtime ritual of showering, brushing my teeth, and settling in for some tv time before bed. I'm searching for my desired channel when a beep sounds from my phone. A message flashes on my screen.

Whoever knows me, knows I am busy watching Glee at this time of night. I hate being interrupted, especially when I am enthralled with Matthew Morrison. Mr. Shu is my favorite. Just as Rachel tries to flirt with Finn again, in the practice room, singing of love, I am answering the phone. "Hello?" My annoyance shines through.

"Hey, Serena," a male voice answers from the other end of the line. "It's me."

Me who? I pull the phone away from my ear, glancing at the number. Nope, not a number I recognize.

"Serena? It's me, Mitch"

Oh. My. God. My eyes widen, and I bite my lower lip to hold back a gasp of shock. Mitch? I went out with Mitch like, what, two years ago? He ended it so he could date a coke head. Literally, a woman who was addicted to coke. I take a deep breath. What does he want with me?

He breaks the silence and pulls me from my thoughts. "Serena? You there?"

"Why hello, Mitch. Long time no hear. How are things?" I sigh with annoyance from the small talk. "How's Courtney?"

"I'm good. Things are good. I'm back in town. And, I have no fuckin clue how Courtney is. We broke up six months ago. I am calling to see if you are free and maybe want to get together for a drink. Maybe talk, you know, for old times' sake."

I have no idea what I am going to do. If I say yes, will he think I want to get back together?

"Alright. Sure. Why not a drink amongst friends? Where, and what time?"

"Friday night. You know the place. Around seven."

His favorite bar. Shit. I am not prepared for this.

Chapter 14

Serena

When Friday arrives, I ask Sally via Skype to help me find the right outfit and give me her thoughts on my meeting with Mitch. She knew about my breakup with Mitch, and helped me pick up the pieces afterward. He left me in my hour of need, and I thought I loved him. I had a twisted idea of what love was.

I looked past the addiction to pot and how it took over his life. It made a major mess of our relationship and I didn't care. When he was sober and looked at me with those soul clenching eyes, my life was right as rain. When we would sing together something always clicked with us. Our voice melded as one.

Then I developed some problems which led to a couple of surgeries. In the meantime, while the tests were taking place he dumped me. He couldn't handle waiting for me to get better. He went looking and found a new voice to meld with. I became history.

"I don't know if this is a good idea, Serena. I mean, he really hurt you. You have no idea how scared I was. I thought Mitch would have been another downfall, and you would swear off love all together after him."

"I think I am much stronger now than I was back then. Don't you agree?" I check myself in the mirror. "Never mind him, I can handle Mitch. He has no power over me."

"I wish I could go with you. That way, I could make sure he doesn't get under your skin. Why is he wanting to see you after all this time anyway?"

That's a really good question. I have no idea. It's too suspicious. He is having me meet him at the bar he usually performs at. And rather early, too. "I have no idea what his angle is. He said he wants to be friends. Who knows? I guess we shall see."

"Just don't sleep with him."

I feel a tightness around my shoulders.

"Promise me, Serena. Promise. Me." She stares into my eyes, forcing me to blink into submission.

"Alright. Alright." I cackle. "I promise, but I wonder what he'll say when he sees me again?" I glance down at the short plaid skirt skimming my crossed upper thighs and the black satin button-down shirt with two buttons — yes, two buttons — open, accentuating my cleavage. The high-heeled Mary Jane on my right foot is bobbing up and down excitedly. I blow at the copper curl that has fallen from my high ponytail and grin. I look like I belong in some private-school porno.

"Oh, I have an idea, take a screenshot and post it. I'd love to see the reactions you get from everyone." Her eyes narrow with suspicion, and I admit, "Okay, I mean one person in particular." She continues to look at me. "Yes, I mean Conner. Geez, you make me seem like I'm obsessive. For your information, I'm in no way obsessed with his opinion of me or his jealous behavior."

The look she gives could make a cat screech.

"I want to make it look like I don't care." I turn up my nose and wave the idea that this is abnormal behavior away.

"To be a fly on the wall. I don't think this is the best look for going to see an ex, but, hey, what do I know?" She thrusts a fist in the air. "Go get 'em, girl."

I see the concern clear through the screen in her slumped shoulders. I look at myself and agree, this doesn't scream hey, I'm over you; it screams I'm a sex fiend school girl, fuck me, professor. Yeah, not what I need.

"Sal, this is going to take a while. I'll talk to you later."

"Talk to me later? You will see me soon enough. Knock the socks off of Switch and give me the play by play later."

"You know his name is Mitch. See you soon." I click the red button to end the Skype call and soldier on.

An hour later, and I have changed my clothes three more times before finally choosing my best blue jeans-the ones that hug my curves perfectly. The shirt is my favorite shade of lilac, with a V neck that shows just the right amount of the cleavage. My shoes match my top.

I look hot. I look my best self.

Chapter 15

Serena

I arrive at the bar and scan the crowd for Mitch. Spotting him at a small table in the corner, I straighten my posture and lift my chin making my way toward him. He looks the same. Tall, tattoos over strained muscles, and his dark hair shaved short. I have a thing for guys bigger than me in both height and muscles. Oh yeah, and tattoos. They always made me feel smaller when I was big. His eyes dart around, undoubtedly, searching for me, but he hadn't noticed me yet.

Once I get within three feet of him, his gaze locks on me, sliding down my body with hungry appreciation. He smirks and rises from his seat. "If I hadn't seen a recent photo of you, I would never know it was you." He smiles at me and pulls me in for a hug. His face turns into my neck, and I hear a sound from his nose. Did he just sniff me?

"Did you just sniff me?" I laugh in surprise.

"Yeah, I guess I did. Old habits die hard, Serena." He holds my hands out and scans me up and down. "You look hot, my dear. Too hot. I am so glad you were able to see me." He gestures for me to sit down across from him at the table. "Drink?" He raises, his beer. "Don't worry, I'm buying." His eyes squint, and his proverbial lightbulb went off. "Hard cider, ok? You know they don't do girlie drinks here."

I nod my head, and he orders me the alcoholic apple goodness.

"Alright, so...I have a favor to ask. I know you wouldn't do this under normal circumstances, but I need a singer for tonight's gig. My singer bailed on me, and I was wondering if you would stand in."

"This is why you wanted to see me? Really? You could have asked me over the phone," I huff, standing from my chair. He grabs my wrist and stares up at me with a sad look in his eyes: like the one I remember giving in to so many times before. I blow a piece of hair from my face and decide to stay. If I am going to help him, he will be playing my old set. The songs I am good at. Nothing surprising. "Alright. But only, because I would love to see the guys again." I shake my finger. "Listen carefully, it's my old set, or I walk."

"You got it. I promise. We go on at ten. You need to go warm up?"

"You know I do." There is a different feeling in the air. The surge of excitement changes my expectations. This may be the new path I've been looking for.

This was going to be so much different than when I performed two years ago. Back then, I was much heavier and moving around on stage for me was near to impossible. An ornately framed mirror behind the bar catches my eye as Mitch heads through the Employees Only door next to the far side of the bar. I examine my image and take a deep breath, considering my sudden fall down the rabbit hole.

My fingers click away at one last update on my social media account— one of several since I met Mitch and agreed to sing for the band two hours before. Watching the band tune their instruments and layout the remaining gear, I grin, pleased with myself. I may have mentioned a time or two on Facebook that I was performing with the band Erroneous Charge. Part of me wanted to see Conner show up and part of me was terrified. I know there is nothing going on there, but I feel wrong with two exes in one space. If Conner shows up, it will feel like "The Hall Of Serena's Exes."

The band takes the stage, and my knees begin to shake. I can do this. I repeat this mantra over and over again. I CAN DO THIS! I step onto the platform, and the drummer taps out a rhythm, prompting me to join in. I start singing of a heartbreaker, dream maker. After our third rock song, I let myself go and kick off my heels then jump around on stage. The crowd loves it, like my enjoyment fuels theirs. The applause is infectious. I am speechless.

Glancing to my right, I see Mitch smiling at me with a gleam of pride in his eyes like old times. My heart takes a dip, but not like it used to. I can now look at him and see he isn't meant for me.

I keep peering out over the audience's heads, toward the entrance. I guess, I was hoping to see Conner. I start singing the next song, "Want To" by Sugarland. The yearning of a relationship, and wanting it if he wanted it, held in the air. I am losing hope, giving up on the possibility of Conner showing up.

Minutes later, as I sang the last bridge, my eyes sweep the audience again. There he is. My cheeks burn. Conner is here. I smile a little wider. Strut a little more. I breeze through the set knowing he is here for me.

When the set is over, I put my shoes back on and rush off the stage. Before I hit the last step, I am face to face with him. My breath catches and I'm taken aback. His hair is in a 'I just rolled out of bed' style. His shirt clings tight to his body, showing off his muscles. Is that a new tattoo under the sleeve of his black shirt? The ink peeking past the trim appears fresh. A strand of entwined barbed wire wrapped around his bicep. It is hot. My fingers twitch, fighting the urge to touch his marked muscle.

I try not to seem affected when he stares at me. "So, Con, what are you doing here?"

"I saw there was a band playing down the street on Facebook. Funny, I think it may have been on your page. I said 'hey, what the hell?' I'm gonna go see my good friend, Serena, perform." He uses air quotes to emphasize the words good friend. He then brushes the hair around my ear and kissed my cheek slowly. The spark of his lips feels as if he is staking a claim on me. His gaze lifts to a spot behind me, and he nods, "Hey, I'm Conner, and you are?"

"Mitch." His hand comes out for a shake, but the tone in his voice not at all polite. "I'm Mitch." The arm-wrestling match continues until one breaks free from the shake. Conner scowls. Mitch sneers at Conner as if he's intruding. He crosses his arms and sizes up Conner as if he were nothing more than a pup in a big dog's world. Conner narrows his eyes and broadens his shoulders in response. Mitch hooks his arm around my waist as if calling dibs on me. "How do you know Serena?"

"Serena and I went to high school together." His tone is full of jealousy. "We sorta hung out a lot in our senior year."

He stares down his competition and places his arm around my shoulders. This is spaghetti western, high noon moment. The dustbowl is rolling by. "Who the hell are you?"

What's this, a pissing contest? Men marking me like territory up for grabs? I don't know if I should be flattered or if I should break up the battle royal. Let the battle begin.

"Conner, this is Mitch. Mitch and I briefly dated for a year or so, until I got dumped for coke-head Courtney." Mitch's head jerks in my direction, and regret softens his stubborn features. "I did him a favor. His singer bailed, and he needed someone to sing." I stare into Conner's eyes as to say, I am NOT with him. Never ever. Never. EVER.

As we start to walk away for my break in between sets, I hear a voice over the speakers from the stage. "Are you ready for round two?" The booming voices echo off the audience. I look as I sucked a sour lemon, took a deep breath, did a one eighty and feigned a smile. Without thinking my feet drag back to the stage. "Are you all having a good night?" The crowd swells with cheers and Mitch introduces me. "Please help welcome back to the stage... Serena."

I roll my eyes, feign a smil,e and approach the stage. That was the quickest break between sets. I'm handed the tambourine and know exactly what song he is choosing. Mitch turns his head slightly to the right so I get a clear view of his eyes as he wiggles them. Shit! Nothing like making a play for me in front of everyone.

Mitch has his favorite acoustic guitar gingerly strapped around his shoulder. "This song is a special one. A classic straight from the nineties. Here we go..." He looks over to the drummer and gives a nod. The click of the sticks over his head count to three.

He sings in my direction, "Hold on little girl..." I shake my tambourine to the beat. I smile for the crowd. I shoot Mitch the side eye. The onslaught continues on about waiting in a line and wanting to be with someone. He's laying it on thick and I don't know if I should be flattered or annoyed. Conner and I pass glances and I see flames forming around his head. His aura has shades of oranges and reds.

The final song of the set ends and I've had enough for the night. I make a beeline for the door. I don't care who is here or how this looks. I need out of this mess. I rush out the bar and hunch down on my knees. My lungs constrict as I gulp deep breaths.

I feel a tap on my shoulder. "Look Mitch I'm done for the nigh..." I turn to look up and see Conner looking back at me. I suddenly feel at ease.

"You were incredible." My body betrays me and rises up. "I may want to punch his face, but I will hold myself back." My smile is weak, and a sliver of my broken heart is falling back into place.

I see Conner's expression change and I turn in the direction he is facing. Conner grabs my hand and butterflies take to the air in my gut.

Mitch, out of breath from trying to catch up, makes an effort to steal my attention. "Serena, would you consider coming back to the band? We could use your voice."

I start to look uneasy and unsure. Conner takes a hint. "Well, Serena, are you ready to go now? I promised you dinner tonight. I know it's a little late, but I would still love to get something to eat."

Thank you, Lord, for helping me get the heck out of here. There was too much testosterone in the air. The two were ready to bite off each other's head to claim me as their prize. I link my arm in the crook of Conner's elbow. We look at each other and we turn to leave.

"I'll think about it." Wanna play games Mitch? Let's play. "I'm not sure if I'll manage it with my schedule. I'll call you." I give Conner an apologetic smile.

At a diner near my apartment, we sink into a red leather booth, drinking coffee and sharing disco fries. I can't believe I am eating these. There will be extra time in the gym for this splurge. I stare out the window and take a deep breath.

"Thank you again for getting me out of there. Mitch is someone in my past that should really stay there. Though, his offer is tempting. I really want to get back to singing. It could be a good way to come back."

"Should I stay in your past too, Serena?" Conner gazes at me with eyes so deep, I could lose myself in them. They are so full of emotion — yearning, sadness, defeat — with a glint of the boy I once knew. I can't get enough of them.

"I didn't say you." I take yet another breath and sighed. I resign to the facts. "I always thought that, maybe someday, you would find me. I don't know why; I just did." Tears streak down my face, and I can't hold it in anymore. The flood gates open up. "If you and I try again, I would never know if it was because you want me because I'm socially acceptable now that I'm not the fat girl, or is it pity for how you treated me back then."

"Serena, I don't care what you look like. I would care for you at three hundred pounds or at a hundred twenty pounds. My stupidity let me believe being with you was wrong. I will never let it happen again. Please, let me prove it to you. I don't normally beg, but here I am, begging you for another chance."

I reign in my tears, sniffling and wiping the wetness from my eyes as I consider his request. "Well, we can try dating casually. Nothing serious. Just to see where this goes." A smile creeps over my face. "I don't know if I can be intimate with you yet. I need a little time. See how this goes." I could so go there in a heartbeat, but I need his proof. I need to know he wants the woman inside.

"I'll give you all the time in the world, so long as I can be with you in any way, you'll allow me." He reaches across the table and squeezes my hand. As he and I scoot out of our booth and exit the diner, he arches an eyebrow at me while lacing his fingers with mine. The touch feeling so right. "Now tell me more about this Mitch before I become seriously jealous and go back to hit him."

There is no way in hell I'm letting him anywhere near Mitch. This is a powder keg waiting to explode.

To pacify, I proceed to tell him the history of Mitch and I. By the time I finished, his nostrils flare and his jaw twitches. "Your mother couldn't stand me, yet she liked you dating a "pot head"? He shook his head. "I don't get it."

"You were around me when it was convenient, and no one would find out." I stare at him. "You had a reputation to protect. Couldn't be seen with the school's fat girl, no matter how awesome you claimed her to be."

We sit in silence for what seems like forever, before he finally interjects. "Look, are we ever going to talk about it? I need to tell you something."

"Tonight, is not a good night to talk about it. We will, but not tonight." I have something to tell him too, and I have no idea how he will react in regards to what I need to say. My silent fear of the truth he never knew. Why my mother truly disliked him. He better be ready when I tell him.

Chapter 16

Serena

Finally, I'm not going to be alone in this big apartment. I overnighted Sally the keys two weeks ago so she could get settled in if I wasn't home. I am hanging out in my house, still in my pajamas, reading, when the noise of a turned key startles me. I jump and see the door open followed by a huge suitcase swinging over the threshold. Sally is finally here.

The suitcase drops with a loud thud. She stretches out her arms and shouts to me, "Honey, I'm home," She begins to chuckle at me. "You better have my coffee ready and my bedroom slippers waiting in hand."

After I help her lug in the few bags she still has in the car, I introduce Sal to her new home. She likes the apartment and squeals happily when she sees her room.

"Welcome home." With a British accent, I inform her, "Dinner is promptly at six. Please, refrain from smoking in the apartment. Are there any questions?"

Sal rolls her eyes and flops down on her new bed. "Please tell me we are hanging here tonight?"

"Of course. I have a Chinese take-out menu- one that delivers- and Muriel's Wedding. It is going to be a fantablulous night."

A few hours later, all the boxes are in the apartment, and we decide on our "mega" Chinese meal. After settling in for some steamed dumplings and really good wine, we pop in the movie. We bop around when Rhonda and Muriel start lip syncing to "Waterloo." Brought back to our teenage years, we giggle. Over our bouts of laughter, I shout, "Sal, I love when Rhonda tells Muriel's "friends" off."

The movie progresses, and when Rhonda becomes paralyzed and is confined to a chair, Sally throws a napkin at me and asks jokingly, "Will you take care of me when I am in a wheelchair and in denial?"

"Please, oh please, tell me that's the wine talking. I will protect you with my life. You are the sister I never had." This is an absolutely morbid conversation to be having.

"So, you hung out with Conner." Subject changed. "How did it go? Did he help you remember the 'good feeling'?" She lifts her eyebrows up suggestively.

I tell her about the whole confrontation between Mitch and Conner. She seems pleased to hear Conner got jealous and helped me out of the situation. "No. We are going to be friends, try dating casually. I don't know if he sees me as the desperate fat girl in high school, or this thinned out version now. Either way, I will never know how he truly feels. I don't know what is the right choice."

She ignores my last comment. "How long, Serena? How long has it been since the last time you were intimate with anyone? I bet your vagina has cobwebs due to low usage."

I shove her arm, then playfully throw a fortune cookie at her. "For your information, there hasn't been anyone in that capacity since..." I trail off, thinking hard about my last time. Surely, it couldn't have been so long ago. I mean Mitch was two years ago, and there was some heavy flirting with the Starbucks guy, but it hadn't panned out. All I got there was a venti latte when I ordered a grande and maybe a free cookie here and there.

"You don't have to say anything. I see it in your face. We will go out tomorrow night. I am here now, and I will not let you grow anymore cobwebs on your lady bits." She breaks into laughter. "Lady bits… I kill me."

"Have I told you how happy I am to have you here? I love you, Sal." I squeeze her into a hug then rest my head on her shoulder.

"You keep telling me. I love you too Serena. Since we've had our hallmark moment, I think it's time to hit the hay."

Chapter 17

Serena

The next few week flies by. I finish my voice overs for the season, and am now on hiatus until the Fall. I am still planning my audition schedule to see if I could land a gig on a show for the summer. I call my agent, and they say they have a couple of possibilities for me but nothing concrete. I even grab a Backstage paper to see if there are any classes, auditions, anything listed. I can't see myself sitting at home with nothing to do every day. I even consider getting certified to teach yoga.

Already feeling "cabin fever," I call Ivan to see if he can use my help preparing for his audition. I sweeten the deal by offering if so, Sally will tag along when I come. It might be bribery, but I'm desperate and I don't want to give him a chance to refuse her attendance.

"I guess it's alright if she comes. It's not like it's a closed class or lesson. Bring whomever," he permits nonchalantly.

Later that evening, I drag Sally kicking and screaming to the studio.

"I have no idea why your friends with him. He is such an annoying prick." She enters the building, scowling over her shoulder at me and grumbling, "He is way too into himself to really give a—" She bumps into a hard chest.

"Hey, Sally. What don't I give a shit about?" Ivan places his fists on her hips to steady her attempted retreat.

"Oh, Ivan. A pleasure as always." She tucks a lock of hair behind her ear and smooths out her rumpled shirt. Finally, she offers her hand for a shake, which he accepts.

I see the awkwardness and interject, placing myself between them. "Ivan, I'm ready to work. Do you have your camera set up? Maybe you can teach Sally a few things too." I wink at him, hoping to break the tension in the room.

"Look, I am here for Serena. Mainly to watch her dance. Sorry, buddy, I don't think you are that special with that foreign accent and those dance moves." She rolls her eyes, seeming unenthused.

"Oh really?" He approaches Sally and extends his hand. "May I?"

She puffs a stray hair out of her face and shrugs. "I guess so. If you really must." She slaps her hand into his, refusing to go easy on him. With a few frame corrections, Ivan molds her into the dance pose for a Waltz. He waits for the right beat then guides her across the floor. It takes a moment for Sally to get the hang of it. She doesn't seem keen on letting him lead her around. I know she hates not being in charge. I can see the inner struggle on her face as she finally let's go. And, wow, my best friend is absolutely graceful. It brings tears to my eyes. Something changes in her demeanor in those few minutes, like a flower opening for the sun.

Then Ivan opens his mouth. "See, what happens when you submit to me, Sally? Beautiful things happen."

Oh shit. Did he just say submit? He better be ready for the onslaught.

Sally's body stiffens, and she digs her heels into the floor until they stop. "Submit? Submit? I would never submit to you. I don't submit. I was being kind in following your lead."

I sit on a bench at the edge of the studio floor, laughing and shaking my head. My attention gets pulled away from the two of them arguing like an old married couple by a chirp from my phone. I retrieve it from my purse and find a text from Conner. My heart flutters.

> **Conner:** Hey. You busy?
> **Me:** Yeah, at the dance studio with Sal and Ivan. Why?
> **Conner:** Who is Ivan? Another boyfriend?

I glace at the wall-to-wall mirror and see this devilish gleam in my eyes. Wow someone is a little pea green with envy. Even if I wanted to, I won't play around with him.

> **Me:** No, just a friend. Don't be jealous. YOU have no reason to be. You are just a friend too, remember.
> **Conner:** Do you want to hang out?

I quickly call to Sally, "What are we doing tonight? Conner wants to hang."

"I don't know. You want to check out the movies? Maybe the new Ben Affleck movie is playing. Oh, wait, how about a foreign film or maybe something he would so hate?" She smirks with delight.

Ivan chimed in, "Am I missing something here?"

I keep scrolling through the phone looking at movie times and locations on the different apps. "Conner texted me and asked what Sally and I are up too," I answer.

"Ok. So, you are going to torture him with a foreign film with possible naked people and sex? Oh. No. Serena. I am not one to dog my species, but I remember you telling me the story of what happened in school, and I have the BEST solution. There is a movie that was just re-released. I got the perfect cinema gem. Titanic in 3D. Nothing says agony more than DiCaprio."

Sally smiles. "I can't believe I am saying this, but Ivan is right; we must go to Titanic. And the best part... you can tell him we're going since he ruined it oh so many years ago for you."

"Sal, you remember the story?" I look at her, amazed.

"How can I forget it?"

Conner had finally taken me out on a real date. It was across town and away from prying eyes. No one would likely be seeing Titanic, which was already out for months, the same weekend the big blockbuster of the spring was releasing. We thought we were safe. I remember sitting in the passenger side not needing to hide. Singing to the radio like there is not a care in the world. We held hands and just enjoyed being in each other's company.

I remember feeling alive, but also waiting for the other shoe to drop.

I was right the other shoe did drop. His group of friends showed up and he automatically distanced himself from me. I heard some words said as I ran out of that theater. There goes Sidecar Serena. I see she didn't get stuck in her seat.

Another voice shouts I didn't know blubber could run so fast. Quick get that on you tube. I never heard a word of defense from Conner as I ran out of the theater.

"You know Sally I was fortunate there was a bus stopping in front of the theater at that moment, otherwise, I would have been stuck there." I wipe my eyes with the back of my hands.

"Serena, you cried in my room for HOURS," she enunciated the word. "And, now, it's time for some payback." Sally and I nod our heads in agreement.

Ivan chimes in and proceeds cautiously, "Serena, I love you. Can you explain to me why you let someone treat you like that? You are such an awesome person. I don't get the self-torture."

I shrug my shoulders resigned to admit my truth. "I guess it was just something I dealt with. Whenever we were alone, he was such a different person. And I could see the internal conflict he was dealing with every time." I sigh.

Chapter 18

Serena

We made it to the theater on time. The four of us climb to the top row. Unsure who to sit by, I nudge Conner ahead, and choose a seat between him and Sally to keep them from arguing over me. I think, for a brief second, to place myself between Sally and Ivan to keep them from arguing. Then, I realize Sally and Ivan can handle each other. I lower into my seat wanting to be near Conner.

He smells so good. Smells were always my thing. My eyes roam over him, taking in how delicious he looks in jeans and a burgundy V-neck sweater. I can't help it as my skin flushes. I smile, "Thanks for agreeing to see Titanic with us."

"I agreed to this because I owe you for ten years ago." He looks me straight in my eyes. Conner's expression is sullen and downtrodden. When he notices me staring, his expression changes in an instant. The flirt is back again. "Though, I can't promise I'll behave."

With his hint of naughty promises, a jolt of need awakens in my core. I grin and turn to Sal, fanning away the heat rising to my face. Friends! Conner and I need to stay friends.

Oh, my god. Those words make me shiver. Why does my body automatically react to him? How could

I agree to friendship? I bite my crooked finger, wishing the sting could ease my desire to be more than friends. Images of what I want flood my brain. All I want to do is kiss his lips. Kiss him everywhere.

"Conner, you need to let it go. She isn't here for you this time."

I glower at Sally.

I might be having a change of heart. So, his smile is starting to get to me again. So what? Nothing. I don't know if I can do the friend thing.

The movie theater starts to darken, and the previews roll. Sally and I drool over the trailer for Magic Mike. Wow, those guys are hot and they dance.

Ivan leans forward, catching my attention with the disapproving shake of his head.

I lean to my right and ask, "Sal, is it getting hot in here?" I giggle at Ivan as he plops back in his seat pouting.

"I think so. I think we need some water." She glares at Ivan. "So, dancer boy, can you do that?" She points to the screen, and Ivan laughs.

"Do you really want to know? Maybe I can, maybe I can't. Would you like me to audition for you?" Ivan winks when Sally bites down on her bottom lip, speechless.

The movie begins, and before I know it, it's the scene, the one with the necklace. The one where Jack draws Rose. I feel a hand grab mine, and it isn't Sally's. I turn to my left and see green eyes burning into mine.

Conner twists in his seat to face me. His other hand tilts my chin up, coaxing me closer. He kisses me. Not some peck on the cheek either. It's like he wants to devour me.

I pull away, gasping. I am glad it is dark because I'm sure my cheeks flushed a bright rose when he whispers, "I've been itching to do that all night. I want to kiss you during the movies to make up for the time I missed out on before."

I think I just melted. If he was trying to break my defenses down, this was a big start.

I know now that we are older. Maybe, just maybe, this time it's different.

I start to cry when I see Rose let go of Jack's hand. By now, Conner's arm is curved around me, and my head is on his chest. He reaches in his pocket and retrieves a handkerchief, offering it to me. I sniffle and accept the swatch of fabric. "A hankey? Who still carries those?" I dab my eyes, smiling. "I'm so sorry this movie gets me every time." Hearing a sniffle behind me, I turn to face Sally. "Are you alright?" She nods, light glistening off her wet cheeks. I guess we both react the same way when it comes to this film.

The end credits begin, and Celine Dion's voice breaks into song over the speakers. Sal and I sing along, over exaggerating the lyrics. We are pulling attention in our direction. I grab Sally's hand as if to serenade her and belt out, "You're here there's nothing I fear." We're laughing. Sal takes her fist to her chest like she's touched by my performance. At this point, I am laughing so hard tears are streaming down my face. "That woman knows how the heart goes on!"

I slide my phone from my pocket and press the on button. A few text messages scroll across my screen. One of them is from Mitch saying he needs to talk about something. Whatever for, I have no idea. I really don't have anything to say. I text back quickly, sorry kind of busy.

"Who was it?" Conner questions, peeking over my shoulder. The jealousy wafts over him in waves.

Emotionless, I reply. "Mitch. Why?"

Conner eyes me like I took his favorite toy away. "So, are you going to talk to him?"

"I guess I need to. I should see what's going on." I rest my hand over Conner's heart. When he opens his mouth to speak, I shush him with my finger on his lips. "And before you say anything, no, I'm not interested in him."

"Good, because I don't intend to share you with anyone else." He snags my forefinger into my mouth and sucks it.

My breath halts, and I begin to tremble. Once the realization of what he said settles in my barely coherent thoughts, I harden my dazed features. "Share me? Share me?" I can feel my face get warm, and my blood pressure rises. I'm disgusted. "You can't share me because I am NOT yours." I spin on my heels to walk away, but he grabs my arm and turns me around to face him, again.

"You were always mine. Even when we were apart, you were always in my thoughts." His hands caress my face. His green eyes bore into mine. "I said, if I was lucky to have you in my life again, I would make it right. I would finally make you mine." Conner releases my face, and turns his back to me.

We walk out of the theater hand in hand. I face him and let go. The cool night air magnifies the absence of his warm touch. "I was selfish before. I kept you hidden from everyone. No one but you has ever held my heart. Please, Serena, I'm begging, please. I am done being friends. I'm not patient, waiting for you to wake up and realize we are meant to be. I want more. More for us. Give me more."

I am stunned into silence. He places his hands on my cheeks again and draws my mouth up to his. His kiss is so soft, gentle.

I don't know how to react. In the moment, my heart and my body betray me, surrendering to the memory of what we used to be. I meet his mouth with a hunger, a need, a passion that long ago left me. Here I am vulnerable, exposed, and wanting.

I take a deep breath and sigh. I shouldn't but I am. "Alright, Conner. Alright. I will give you this one chance. I don't know why but you have worn me down." I gave in to my desires. Shit, here I go, down the rabbit hole. "I want to be yours again. I can't keep fighting it, but I'm not going to make this easy. Don't mess this up for me. For us. I don't know if I can handle the fall again." I'm hoping this leap of faith is going to be worth it. An expression of what I believe is euphoria spreads across his face and then to mine.

"You won't be sorry. I promise you. This time is going to be so much better." He takes my forearms in his hands and stretches me out. I catch the gleam in his eyes. Pulling me into a hug, he muffles into my hair. "It's you and me. And now this is settled, I guess you can call Mitch back to see what he wants."

I snuggle into Conner's side and press the number in Mitch's text before holding the phone to my ear. He answers quickly, already knowing it's me. "Hey there, sexy. I have a proposition for you."

105

My brows pinch together. "What is it?" I stare at Sal, Ivan, and Conner as Mitch lays out his proposal. I bob my head up and down and flash a teeth-showing grin to my crew. This is an offer too good to pass up. "Alright. Let me mull it over, and I will call you back in a couple of days. Thank you. Bye." I hit end and stand there stunned. "Mitch says they have officially fired the coke-head ex from their band and have requested that I permanently take over as lead singer. They know my only vice is chocolate, and I live a pretty clean life. Well, minus the occasional drink." My ramblings continue. I pause and lock eyes with Sally. Without a word, we squeal in excitement, jumping up and down.

Conner, on the other hand, doesn't appear to share in my excitement. To soothe his unease, I give him an answer that should pacify his jealously. "I did say I need to think about. As you heard. I know I can trust myself, and yes, the band does mostly covers, but at least they don't travel. This is a once-in- a-lifetime opportunity." Conner stares at the dirt on his shoe. To keep his trust, I continue with my speech. "Conner, I will tell him no if you want me too."

"I know I want you to tell him no, but what kind of person would I be to stand in your way? I just got you to agree to take me back. You make the decision, and I'll go along for the ride." He grabs my hand and kisses the inside of my wrist. The possessiveness layered under his jealously sends shiver up my spine. "I care too much for you."

I lick my lips then tear my attention from Conner to look at my best-friend. "Sal, what do you think?" She is the one who knows me the best. She is the only one who has been to Hell and back with me and knows exactly what I am thinking. "I know I have final say in my own decisions, but I need your voice of reason right now."

She winks at me. "I say go for it. What do you have to lose? You are on a break, so the time is there. I say do it for fun, but if he tries anything," she glances at Conner then back to me with a hint of the tough teenage-girl with secrets I remember from years ago, "break his nuts."

I decide to take the leap of faith and go for it. I send a text to Mitch, accepting his offer.

He replies that rehearsals start later this week, and I couldn't be happier. "I feel like celebrating," I shout, tugging Conner and Sal's hands as Ivan follows us back to the car.

"I'm so proud of you Serena. I know you wouldn't have done this a year ago," Sally exclaims. Tears well in her eyes.

"Tell me I'm not crazy." I was told if something scares you should run toward it or you will always wonder what if. I must be crazy. This is a terrifying move.

"Serena, you are definitely not crazy. Maybe coocoo for Cocoa Puffs sometimes, but completely psychotic? Nah..." Sally studies my expression for a moment. I watch her eyes move back and forth, but she smiles when she sees me smiling back at her.

My pace up the steps to my third-floor apartment is a flurry of a rush and purpose. With key in hand, I unlock the door. Conner grazes the small of my back with this hand and leads me inside.

Hesitating outside the door, Ivan peers inside our apartment, brows furrowed, then nods as if answering a question, he was mulling over in his head. "Sal, I was thinking. Do you want to go out for a little bit with me? Maybe grab a pizza? Or a burger?" Ivan steps closer to Sally and winks at her. I watch the two intently, hoping Sally gets the idea and accepts his invitation.

I take a deep breath when Sally finally answers. "Sure, let's go. I could use a walk. It's a beautiful night, and I am a little hungry." She smiles at Ivan. I swear I can see the ice melting between them. "I'm glad you're buying."

"Wait a second I never said I was paying, Mishka."

Sally and I glare at him like he's grown two heads."

"Come on, Russian. I'm mooching off you." She smirks, looking right at Ivan. "And you better deliver."

The two glances at me with playful expressions before turning to leave. "Later, Serena," Sal says, waving over her shoulder as they walk away.

"Yeah." Ivan chortles, holding his hand up for a brief good-bye gesture. "Later, Serena."

I close the door, and the click when the locking mechanism engages with the frame is deafening. We are alone. Our breathing soon becomes the only sound I can focus on.

Chapter 19

Serena

"So, Serena…," Conner winks at me. "It appears we are all alone. What are we to do?" He bridges the gap and smiles. The passion and heat in his gaze make me suddenly breathless. He reaches behind my head, squeezes the clip in my hair and pulls it out. My red locks tumble down and frame my face. He peppers kisses up my neck toward my ear. "I always wondered what it would be like to get you back. I have prayed for this moment. You, Serena, you… are who I want." He reassures me, "You could be four hundred pounds, and I still would care for you. The person you are inside is what makes you the woman I want. Don't ever forget that, my dear." He trails kisses along my jaw, then to my neck, and finally back up to seal his mouth over mine.

This kiss could go on forever, and I wouldn't stop it. I am oblivious to everything going on. I want this feeling to last forever.

He breaks the kiss, and a smile stretches across his lips. "Serena, I know I want to, but do you? I mean, want to?" He wriggles his eyebrows, referencing exactly what my body already expresses.

I can't speak, but I can show him. I link my hand in his and grin seductively, tugging him toward my bedroom. I quickly turned around and with my other hand, crook my finger with a "come here" motion. A secret longing, I am with holding is resurfacing, and the courage I am feeling opens Pandora's box. I drop his hand, and as I turn back around, I remove my top and drop it on the floor like it was nothing.

I can hear Conner make a low growl, pausing his steps. The only sound is our deep breaths. I hear the rushing of feet behind me. His warm arms snake around my middle, obliterating the space between us — my back to his muscled chest. As we make it to my sanctuary, he gently sucks on my neck between soft kisses. "Mmm, you taste good. Like spice and vanilla. If you taste this good here, I bet you'll taste amazing elsewhere else." He traces a finger from the divot between my collarbones, along my rapidly rising and falling breastbone, and ends in a small, teasing circle around my naval. I moan softly. Wetness soaks into my panties while the excitement and anticipation of having his hands on me wracks my senses.

My cheeks flush as I wiggle free from his embrace, needing a moment to gather my wits. I cross the room to turn on my bedside lamp. If this was going to be anything like what I am imagining in my head, I need to see him, want to see every bit of our bodies moving with each other. I spin around and unfasten the clasps on my shoes, taking them off one by one and letting them drop to the floor. Keeping my eyes on his, I shimmy out of my pants and notice his pupils dilating at the sight of me standing in my underwear, exposed.

My gaze roams down his body, landing on the growing bulge behind his zipper. I lick my lips, my mouth watering. He counters my teasing by slowly unbuttoning his shirt and shrugging it to the floor. My breaths quicken as I memorize each beautiful valley and mound of his torso. I must say the gym does his body good. With a pleased grin, he toes off his shoes, then tugs his zipper down and pushes his pants to his ankles before stepping out of them. He rests his hands on his sculpted hips, watching me like a hawk. God Bless BVD.

I saunter over and skim a finger inside the band of his underwear, pulling it away from his waist just enough to make a light thwack sound when I let it go. His muscles clench in response. "Show me yours, and I'll show you mine," I tease.

He chuckles, ending with a light-hearted sigh. "I remember saying those same lines at one time. This time is going to be different. I know I was your first. I know I was not the best then, but, honestly, time has been my friend. It taught me one thing in particular."

"And what is that?" My smile becomes timid and shy as I my eyes drift up and down. His abs are definitely showing a six pack. I want to lick every ridge on his body. The tattoo on his left arm creeps from his shoulder to his forearm. Lines of black crisscross, intertwining around each other to create an intricate pattern.

Reaching for my hand, he lifts it to his mouth and kisses my middle knuckle, drawing my attention back to his face. "Ladies first. In all aspects." He winks at me. He steps forward and jerks me into him. "Now, while I am rather enjoying the view, I really need this to go." He points to my bra then slides his fingers around the edging on the front. I raise my hands to the clasp between my breasts but he stops me. "Please I have waited ten years for this. Allow me."

"Alright, hot stuff, have at it." I move my hands away.

"This is not the time for jokes. I need to be inside you. To taste you. To make sure you know, without a shadow of a doubt, that I am in this. To know you will be mine." After fidgeting my bra loose, his eyes lock on my fully naked chest, and he swallows hard. In a flash, he leaves me, yanks his wallet from his pant-pocket, then fumbles to get something out of the inside flap.

Ah... a condom. I haven't had to buy those in a while. Yes, it's been a little break.

I never expected sex to be so good. Conner and I were so young and inexperienced. We were lucky to know tab a went into slot b. Since then, I thought of it as a way to feed those urges and to quickly satisfy me. I never truly thought I would ever be with the right person. Sally always told me that it would be different when I was, but I hadn't found him yet.

I turn to climb on the bed, but I'm stopped in my tracks by Conner scooping me off my feet like I weigh nothing and gently laying me on my back. He reaches back grabbing the condom, and places it on my nightstand. He moves above me, placing one hand on either side of my head and urging my knees to open so he can settle between my legs. He feathers hot kisses in a path down my neck, chest, and stomach until he reaches my slick folds.

He leans back, inspecting my most private parts for a moment, and bites his bottom lip with a groan. The sweet pressure of his finger sliding down my crease before sinking into me forces a jolt of pleasure to flood my body. A moan escapes my parted lips.

"Babe, you are so wet. You must be excited at the thought of what I am going to do to you. I'm going to take this as slow as I can, but honestly, I may not last too long." He circles my clit with his finger and lowers his mouth to me. Licking. Tasting. Taking what's his. What was always his. He lifts his head, panting. "I was right. You do taste good everywhere. Not like I remember. I remember you tasting sweet, but not this heavenly." Conner doesn't wait for me to reply. He dives back in, flicking his glorious tongue over every sensitive nerve ending between my trembling thighs.

The pleasure is too great. I can't get any words out. It is like my brain has short-circuited. I ride the wave as my orgasm builds. My body loses control. My toes curl from this electrifying experience and it's too much. I let the pleasure take over, and I writhe against his tongue.

As I float down from the peak of my climax, the warmth of his palm engulfs my breast and begins to massage me. First, the right side, plucking and kneading until the little pink bud is erect. Then, the left side. He nibbles his way up my mound and over my quivering belly to meet his finger.

"Conner... Conner, I need you inside me. NOW." He doesn't hesitate. I reach over and grab the condom from the nightstand. I rip the wrapper with my teeth and sheath his hard dick. I, honestly, don't remember it being as large back then. Granted, it was ten years ago.

My concentration is honed on getting the damn rubber on as quickly as possible, but I still when his hand rests on my cheek. He caresses his thumb across my bottom lip. I gaze into his eyes and have to take in a deep breath. The lust. The desire. The love. Love? He can't love me so soon. I don't know if I even love him.

That's a lie.

I've always loved him.

I tried to move on from him over the past ten years, but the more I tried, the more he stayed in my heart.

"You're so ready. I want to be inside you now." He slides home.

The sensation of him filling me is delicious. I want to tell him how amazing he feels, but I can't think straight.

He groans, "God, you feel so good. So tight. I haven't felt anything like this since being with you. It's like my body remembers how you feel. My happy place is magically appearing before me."

"This feels so good." It is all I could muster. My brain has left me again.

"This is it. You are mine. You've always been mine. Never forget that."

"Yes, Conner. Yours always. Please, I'm about to cum." I whimper. The consuming tension tightening in my core intensifies.

"I feel it. Let it go. I'm almost there with you."

I'm right on the cusp. Three more thick, long strokes, and I plummet over the edge, screaming out his name. Conner is right behind me. He pumps once, twice, and I feel his pulsating release. He roars through the end, pressing into me as deep as he can go. Breathing heavy, he peers down at me and smiles, smoothing back the hair matted to my sweaty face.

What is that? I feel free. The only thing I can compare this high to is being on stage. He has fucked me speechless. I can't stop the internal grin. The only words I can come up with are, "Well, that was unexpected."

"God, I missed you, Serena. So much. You'll never know how much. I can't take back all the hurt and the years apart, but I promise, from this moment forward, I will never do that again. You are mine. And I think I was always yours. You've always held my heart in your hands."

He pulls out, and I turn onto my side. Cuddling up to my back, Conner wraps his arms around me and squeezes me against his chest. He peppers kisses into my hair. So overcome with emotion, I can't hold back my quiet sobs any longer. They aren't tears of sadness, but tears of joy and blissfulness. I am in heaven. I feel safe and wanted with this man. I haven't ever felt like this for anyone but him. The warmth of his body calms me. We fall into a peaceful slumber.

The next morning, he asks me "So, quick question. I noticed you have a tattoo…," He tickles the Hebrew scrolling on the lower left side of my back with his fingertips. "What does it say?"

"It's a song lyric. It's from one of my favorite songs. The Wheel by Rosanne Cash. The line is 'The truth moves through us, even when we sleep.'"

Eyeing the ink as his fingers trace every swirl and sweep of each letter, he says, "It's beautiful."

"I feel that no matter what happens in life, the truth is always there. You may have hated me on the outside, but the truth on the inside is you liked me. Even as a friend." I pause, noting the regret flickering across his features. "Honey, I never stopped caring for you. I was hurt. Yes, more than you will ever know. I figured, one day, we would grow up and find what is ours rings true."

"Baby, don't ever stop caring about me. I may be a jerk, but this jerk cares deeply. I really, truly...," his voice trails off.

I let it go because it's too soon to speak those words. But he's right, I love him too. I never stopped, and here I am in a bed with him. We're not sneaking around, not hiding the facts about how we feel.

The moment is blissful, until he utters a sentence I don't want to confront. "So, what do you think your mom is going to say when she finds out I'm back in your life?"

"I don't know. She wasn't too happy when she heard I saw you at the reunion. Or the fact that you showed up at the bar the other night. She's Team Mitch." He looks at me with that confused stare he used to give Mr. Hicks in history class. "She liked Mitch and still doesn't understand how that one ended. We'll have to decide when is a good time for a visit, but right now, I think she doesn't need to know." I twist toward him, pressing my naked body to his, and kiss him.

Chapter 20

Serena

After a couple of weeks of rehearsals and shows, I'm still not tired of the new routine. Conner is playing the role of the supportive boyfriend. He's been to all my performances and continues to watch with a protective stance. When Mitch and I perform a duet, Conner scowls and glares so he can get the message across that I'm not to be toyed with.

Even with the male posturing, I'm happy to be in my element. Mitch has approached me on a few occasions about writing with him. I have no idea if I am good at songwriting. I've told him over and over again that I am a singer, not a singer-songwriter.

Meanwhile, Conner keeps asking me to tell my mom we are dating, so she can prepare for when things move forward. She's not going to be happy. How do you explain, sure, he verbally abused me in public, but, hey, he really cares for me and isn't ashamed of me now.

"Are you ashamed of me? I mean, if you are…," he trails off.

"Why would I be ashamed of you? I care about you. I'm only trying to figure out how to explain this to my mom."

"So, you are ashamed of me?"

Is he starting a fight? If so, I will win.

I change my approach and soften the blow. "I didn't say that." Oh, how the roles have changed.

"So, tell her. Call her now." He hands me the phone and spins around heading to the living room. I take the phone and follow him.

Frustrated, I grab his arm. "It's not that simple. This is something I need to tell her in person." I urge him around to face me. "She needs to see my expression. To see that I am happy, and there is nothing to worry about."

"I guess I don't get it." He's fuming.

"Ok, here's why. The last time you hurt me in public, which was the day after the prom, we were all at the theme park. I couldn't fit in the seat for the rollercoaster. You and I, just the night before..." Tears sting my eyes. "Well, let's say I was so mortified I went home. Even Charlie didn't understand what was happening. You remember Charlie?" My voice had a bite of bitterness. "He took me to prom, because you wouldn't be seen with me." The tears flow, down my cheeks, and over my nose. I lick the salt away as the tears meet my lips. "When I arrived home, I ran into my room and locked myself in. I told my mom I would never speak to you again." I huffed out a sarcastic chuckle. If only he knew the real truth. He wasn't ready to know what really happened that day. It was something I didn't recover from for many years. "She didn't like you, but she didn't understand why until she saw my eyes and knew what had happened. My heart was breaking, and all she had to say was, 'I told you this was going to happen.'" I cross my arms over my chest. "So, excuse me if I don't want to be the brunt of her judgement. Then, the rumors started that I slept with someone. 'Why would someone want to sleep with her?' they asked." I point a finger at myself, sniffling back a sob. "Oh, and my personal favorite, 'did you pay someone, or was it a suicide mission?' Ain't that rich." I am in the midst of an ugly cry when Conner tries to hug me. "Don't touch me right now. I don't need your pity," I bark, shoving him away.

"I'm certainly not pitying you by any means. Please, understand that was a different time and place." He shrugs his shoulders and, gently touches my forearms. "I am so sorry. When your mom turned me away all those years ago, I tried to write to you in hopes you would get my letters. Did you ever receive any?"

"No, I didn't." I ask an obvious question. "Why didn't you use email?"

"I was trying to be old fashioned." He pushes a stray hair from my face, forcing me to stare directly into his eyes. "Romantic like in the movies or those books you used to read." I turn away astounded. "Ok, I wasn't totally with the cyber age just yet, and I didn't know how to get your email. I tried to contact Sally a few times, but she ignored me at first. What I did was horrible, especially after what was supposed to be a special time for you. For both of us. I loved you then as much as I love you now."

It takes me a moment to process his words. Did he just say he loved me? He moves closer to me, inch by inch with apprehension. He places his palm on my cheek.

I turn into his touch and smile. Tears flood my eyes.

"Serena." He takes a deep breath, his eyes so full of trepidation and remorse. "Serena, I think I always have. Even from the moment we were sent into that closet. That kiss. That kiss made it over for me. My heart was always yours. It was 'game over' for any other girl. I just wish I handled things differently." He lifts my chin with his finger. "Serena Lila Ashby, I love you, and only you. Don't ever doubt that." He kisses me so passionately I have a hard time catching my breath. His eyes soften as he searches mine when he pulls away. "Please, say something. You're way too quiet."

I stand there for what seems like forever, but is really only mere moments. I'm still trying to process what he is admitting. He said he loved me. LOVED me? That he has always loved me. I know deep down in my soul that I love him. It is the tender moments, after the closet, that I knew he was different. I need him in my life. Why did I wait so long?

"I love you too." There, I said it. My heart will never be the same. The men I dated before him, yeah, I loved them but not this all-consuming love. Like I want to have him every minute of every day. I rub the tears from my face, lean to the side, and grab a tissue from the end table. Throwing my arms out in embarrassment, I shake my head and hiccup a laugh. "Sorry, I've become a blubbering mess."

"As long as they're happy tears, I won't worry."

I call my mom and make arrangements to come home for the weekend. I mention having some news to discuss, and she asks if Sally will be coming with me. I could use the extra support, so I tell mom I'll ask if Sal could join in on the trip before hanging up.

Later, when I invite Sally, she answers, "Sure I can stop by the parental units while we're there too." I blow out a breath, relieved I'll have my best friend with me when I approach mom. We pack overnight bags and jump in the car for the four-hour drive.

Thirty minutes into the trip, I turn down the road music and begin probing. "So, what's going on with you and Ivan?" I bait her.

"Absolutely nothing," she scoffs, rolling her eyes. "He annoys me. He thinks it's funny." She pauses for a moment as if thinking about him a little more fondly than she'd like to. "He's trying to teach me some steps, but I don't think I'm ready. What's going on with you and Conner? He's like over almost every night. Why don't you go to his place so I can have some quiet? Sometimes you're a little noisy."

"Sorry." I glance over and smile. "I'll try to keep the screaming to a minimum. Scout's honor. And you're right, it is a little strange I've never seen his place. I need to rectify that situation." I continue to watch the road and shout curses as cars cut me off.

"Calm down. You aren't driving the Audubon."

"I know, I'm just nervous. I am not looking forward to this conversation. My mom and I don't see eye to eye where my love life is concerned."

"She's still mad at him?"

"Yes, but mad is an understatement. She is still hurt at what Conner did years ago, but I need some answers too. He claims he sent letters. He says he looked for me. Sally, you said he contacted you looking for me. Did you tell him where I was?"

"I cannot lie." She takes a breath. "What I am about to tell you may make you furious, but remember I was only protecting you. Remember your sophomore year in college? Your fall semester..."

"Yeah, how can I forget? I was finally on the Mainstage in a play, and I was seeing that guy, Riley. What was I thinking dating him?" I laugh thinking about the short but cute senior that couldn't do anything without messing it up in the process, even our relationship. "You visited for the weekend so you could see me in the play and try to hook up with someone at the after-party."

"Yeah, that was the time. Well, I had received a call from my mom saying Conner called the house looking for me and to call him at some number. I called him back. He asked me if I had kept in touch. If you were alright. He wanted to know if you were happy. I told him yes and that he should know you moved on for himself. I told him about the play and suggested he see for himself. He said he would be there Saturday night and asked me to save a seat for him. I met him at the theater that weekend, and we watched the entire play together. We were so proud of you. I couldn't believe how much you had grown as an actress."

"Are you telling me he was there? He was there the whole time? I asked you if I was seeing things. I asked if I was crazy with stage fright picturing him there. The lone Gerber daisy on my car windshield with no note. You told me I was crazy. 'How would he know where to find you?', you said." I slap my hands against the steering wheel, shaking my head. "I can't believe you." I pull over at the rest area with tears in my eyes.

He was there. Back then, I would have given anything to see him. I feel distraught.

"That's not all." Sally looked at me with uncertainty. She began to wring her hands.

"It isn't?" Sweat starts to trickle down my forehead. My hands tighten around the steering wheel.

"No. When he and I walked into the lobby, you had your back turned because you were running up to Riley, hugging and kissing him. Conner took one look, and his face fell. He turned to me and told me he was leaving. I was glad. I didn't want you to be hurt again. I was only trying to protect you. You have to believe me. I am so sorry."

"I'm furious. I love you like a sister. We've been through so much together, for far too many years, to let this end us, but right now I really need some quiet and space."

The rest of the ride is silent. I can't begin to pinpoint how to feel. Betrayed comes to mind. All I want to do is take her home. I need to meditate on this. I can't stand lying. Too many times I was lied to, and I was devastated.

I drop Sally off at her parents' house with a little more than a curt goodbye and continue on to mine.

I understand everyone was doing what they thought was best for, but making decisions for me… It hurts. I remember what a sad girl I was, even though I don't want to. I want to move on. My therapist told me the past is the past, and we can learn from it and move forward. Conner is certainly not the same person, and I'm not either. We've both grown and changed with the times. I can't keep living by the past and certainly can't keep letting it dictate how I move through my future. I need to live. I'm a totally different person now. Conner sees that. Why am I so scared of letting him into my heart again?

Chapter 21

Serena

I arrive at my childhood home. My mom is waiting for me on the front stoop. "You're here! You're here!" she shouts, jogging to my car.

I smile and embrace the hug I needed. My stomach twists in a knot, knowing how tough it will be to tell her about my current situation. I need to tell her what was going on though, and hopefully, I'll have her and dad's support.

I grab my bag and follow her into the house. "Hey, dad." I hug my father. They are a little older, but they still look the same from when I was little, only with a bit greyer hair.

"So, what's the reason for the visit little girl?" Dad's gaze searches my face.

Here goes nothing. I rip off the band-aid. "I've started seeing someone." My wringing hands and sheepish grin show off my nerves.

Mom smiles at me, while dad glances to the corner of the room, eyeing the baseball bat.

I roll my eyes and poke playfully at my father's shoulder.

He chuckles, "So, who is he, and why isn't he here with you?"

I walk to the couch and sit. "You see, that's why I am here. I've started seeing Conner again."

"In public this time?" Mom blurts out.

"Whoa, Mom. Harsh much?" She stands stiff as a board across the room with her arms crossed and her face drawn. I feel small. What am I, seventeen again? I cross my arms and legs as I sit on the old, bumpy sofa.

"I'm sorry. I just remember what happened to you the last time. I was worried you were going to hurt yourself." She comes over to sit down next to me and wraps me in her arms. "I love you, and I worry if his feelings are genuine." She switches tactics. When did this start? And what about Mitch? He is such a nice boy. He asked you to sing in his band again. Maybe it's a sign."

"Mom, Mitch is a pothead. I mean, he loves it more than he ever loved me. I never felt for him what I feel for Conner." I share the clean version that started with the reunion.

"Atta girl, make him work for it. He needed someone to make him feel the same way you did all those years ago," dad quips with a laugh.

My phone pings, pulling my attention from my parents to my purse. It is a text from Sally. I go to look at it because I can't stay mad at her for long. She and I have to much history as friends to ignore.

Sally: Did you tell them?

Me: Of course, I did. Having fun on your end?

Sally: Yeah, I guess so.

Mom follows the direction of my fingers tapping on my phone. "Who is that?" She huffs, stands and takes her disapproving mother stance, hands on her hips. "Conner? He can't leave you alone." Crossing her arms and shifting her weight, mom blurts out, "This is too fast, Serena. Way too fast."

I mimic her stance and blow the hair away from my face. "Mom, it's not like I'm marrying the guy, we're just dating. Thanks for believing in me. Thanks for trusting my judgement." I turn and start down the hall on auto-pilot. With phone in hand, I finish my text.

Me: I am going for a walk, maybe try to run the track.
Sally: Walk a mile for me.
Me: OK

I put my favorite running gear on and head out the door. Heading up the street, to the back entrance of the school, I welcomed the chance to run off my frustration.

Happy to discover I have the track to myself; I step onto the green turf and begin my usual stretch routine. With my iPod out of my pocket, I situate my ear buds and search for my running playlist. I choose my first song, make sure it's on shuffle, and set into a steady pace.

I run to get whatever I am thinking of out of my head; Mitch, Conner, Sally, even my mother. They all need to fade away for a while. My feet pound along the rubber track at a rhythm that drowns out my worries, allowing me to get lost in the music blasting through my earbuds.

My eyes follow the long silver slats of bleachers, and my mind wanders back to the very man I was trying to figure out. What would it have been like if we really were out together in the world, in high school? Would he have lost his position and friends in school? Or would I have moved up the social ladder? We'll never know. I used to daydream about being under those bleachers with him, making out. Maybe even a little more. I flush at the thought.

I really need to consider where I want this music thing to go. Do I want the career with the band, or do I want to continue acting? Why can't I do both. I can use this adventure as a change in career or maybe to enhance it. Which is the right answer? I have no idea? All I know is music keeps me sane, so I decide to give the band a shot.

At least one of my problems found a solution here today.

Chapter 22

Serena

I woke in my childhood room to my phone ringing. Normally, I would send it to voicemail so early in the morning, but the caller id said Janet Stowell, Agent. "Serena, are you there?"

"Yeah, I'm here." I stretch and yawn. "What's new?" Glancing around at the cotton candy-colored walls with posters of artwork reminds me where I'm at.

"Good and bad news. Bad news, the cartoon was cancelled. Ratings were low and they want to introduce a new show."

"The good news, is you have been asked to audition for The Next Vocal Thing. A family member of one of the producers saw you singing in the bar, and they want you. I think this could be a good avenue for you, and maybe that band of yours."

The Next Vocal Thing gives singers, musical groups, and duos the chance to compete. Each week, they sing cover songs as well as original pieces. And, like other music competition shows, the public votes.

I ponder the idea for a moment. Am I ready to put myself out there—auditioning on live television— so far out of my comfort zone? "So, they want the band?"

"They want you, but they will take the band.

I continue to weigh my options. The answer is clear, I need to work with the band. I need to work on my writing and collaborating would be in the right direction.

I can depend on Mitch more for the musical support. He understands what I am going through. He knows my personal fears of performing. When I look in the mirror, I still see the heavy girl and not the healthy one everyone else does. The band keeps me from running off the stage in a panic. The choice is a no-brainer. The band and I are a package deal.

"I'll tell them and send you the details," she says before hanging up.

I quickly pack my bags back up and call Sally to tell her to be ready to go home or she can get her own ride.

I message Mitch with information about the audition and when I will be home for a rehearsal. I know he hates reality tv but this is a chance we need to take. If we don't, we may never have this again.

I scream down the hall to my parents to get their attention. I hate to leave like this but I need to get back and prepare for this audition with the band.

Sal and I discuss all the possibilities this will bring for me and the band. This is going to be the best shot we got right now. I don't want to blow it. I don't want to make the wrong choice.

Instead of the usual four hours travel we return in three hours. There is a text from Mitch, the band is waiting. I arrive ready to work.

"The audition is in twenty-four hours gentlemen. Let's get down to business. What song do we choose and what do we wear?"

We enter the audition, and I'm so nervous my stomach is doing flips. I move to center stage, squint past the hot spotlights shining on us, and search for a focal point. The intimidating panel of judges line a long table midway up the stadium-style seats. Cameras protrude from various points around the stage, adding to my anxiety.

"What are you singing," asks Brett Thompson from the band, Hurricane.

I fall straight into fangirl mode and completely forget what to say. I may have worked with some famous people but seeing Brett takes me back to my teen years. Stumbling through my words, I manage to answer, "Hel… Hell… Hello. We are Silver Lining, and we will be singing an original song. I wrote this song to get through a rough moment in my life." I glance over at Mitch. He offers me a smile back. He knows why I wrote the song and told me it makes him sad. He knows most of my history. Enough for him to take what I'd written as a poem and add the perfect music to enhance it, creating something beautiful.

Brett gestures toward us. Pen in hand. "Alright. Let's hear it."

I wait for the beat to pick up, and when the moment is right, I let the notes burst from my mouth. "A tear a day, and I'll be ok. It's not the first time I lost you to her. She must be so special I can see…," I continue on to the chorus. "You say be your friend, but how can I stand by watching you cry. You say there's no end, but don't you know some dreams do have to die."

"Thank you," Brett shouts from beyond the spotlights. "I think we can all say we are impressed, and your songwriting is at a great level." A smile sweeps across his face. "Your lives are about to change. We will see you in NYC."

I can't contain my excitement. I want to hug everyone. Mitch and I look at each other and jump up and down like teenage girls meeting their favorite boy band.

I did it.

We did it.

Still in shock, I can't believe this is happening. I'm finally getting a chance at a real music career. Then, Brett says the words that drop me from my high like I've taken a high dive off a skyscraper and am falling to my death. "I hope you're ready for the ride you're in for lady and gents. The show is going to want to know your history. We will need old photos, interviews with friends, everything."

I look over at Mitch, my breath frozen in my lungs as my heart stutters. This can't be happening.

Mitch and I sit in matching chairs opposite of Frankie Kelly, the producer, and watch him shuffle through our files with indifference. He reminds me of a rat. Thin, slim, and swarmy. Warning bells scream in my head. He asks questions about mine and Mitch's past.

"You are about to be tossed into the limelight. People are going to dig into your past and search for dirt." When we hesitate to answer, he leans forward, a concerned expression on his hollow face. "If we know about everything up front, we can battle it head on."

He watches us closely as if choosing his next words carefully.

I narrow my eyes at the lack of sincerity in his tone. My gut-feeling tells me he's fishing for something.

Mitch squirms in his chair. "Serena and I used to date." His Adam's apple bobs as he swallows what appears to be a large, uncomfortable lump in his throat. He combs his fingers nervously through his dark hair and speaks. "I was into drugs and left Serena for the former lead singer of the group, who was very into drugs, mostly coke. I left her when I wouldn't support her habit and the band voted her out."

This was the first time I had heard this. Wow, this was major.

"The band had me contact Serena and beg her to come back. I didn't tell her the whole story out of fear she wouldn't return."

The producer looked between the two of us and expressed concern. I can't tell if this is something he could spin or is he going to avoid these issues. Cracking his knuckles and turning his head from side to side, he takes a long breath. "Ok. We can see what can be done to suppress that if and when the time comes." Frankie peels his attention from Mitch and looks at me. "What's your story?"

I think about what I could tell him that would satisfy the press for a while. I straighten up, place my hands on the table, and say matter of factly, "I was the fat kid in school, Mr. Kelly. I was heavily bullied. The interesting twist is that I was secretly involved with one of them."

He tilts his head to the side and quirks an eyebrow. "You were what? What kind of sick game was that?"

"To make it even more twisted, I am now involved with him again."

The producer leaned slumps back in his chair with wide eyes, then a slow smirk creeps over his mouth. I could practically see his wheels turning. "This is brilliant! We can work with that for the video packages. Is there anything else I need to know?"

I hesitate for a moment. "No, there's nothing else. I have nothing to hide." I relax back into my seat and look at Mitch, smiling my best pageant smile. There is so much more to this story I could confess, but I have to tell Conner first.

Chapter 23

Serena

Crying is all I seem to do. The sobs keep coming. I leave a message for Conner. I need to explain everything.

It takes me a long time to get over what I did. Time to face the demon. I will be leaving for New York soon, and I need to make sure I am in good place emotionally for the competition.

Explanations need to be made to Conner as to why I disappeared. My goal was to disappear from this Earth back when I was seventeen. I couldn't take the pain anymore. My first instinct was to write a note, take some pills and drift off to a deathful slumber. I couldn't locate the pills, so the kitchen knife acted as a lame substitute.

I had my note all written out to my mom:

> *Dear Mom,*
>
> *I'm sorry. I thought I was strong. I thought I could make it despite the harsh words and bullying. I just can't survive. Sticks and stones do break bones, and words definitely hurt. I feel, in time, you will understand I just want the pain to end. Please don't hate me.*
>
> *I hope someday you will forgive me.*
> *Love Always,*
> *Serena*

I would have gone through with it if she hadn't come home and found me. She stood there and listened to everything I said that day. I still have no idea how she kept her cool through it all. She heard me rant and cry for hours till I finally calmed down long enough to pack a bag and she checked me into the hospital to be evaluated.

My whole life from that moment was never the same. My family never left me alone for years. I had daily check ins with my parents, the RA in my dorm and even Sally. Ongoing therapy to understand what I was needed to heal.

I wipe away splotchy waterworks and walk to my closet to choose an outfit. I shower, change, and spend a little extra time on my hair and makeup. I can't believe I am about to tell Conner the truth. I stand in front of the mirror in a daze. My mind races with all the scenarios of how he will react. Another wave of emotions crashes over me.

Will he be angry that I kept this from him?

Will he blame himself for the disarray my life became because of our time together?

Will it draw him closer?

Either way, if anything gets out, he needs to know first.

I open the door to find Conner sitting in my living room. His back is to me, so he doesn't see me at first. I take in the view. From the back he's perfection. Sporting fitted charcoal slacks and a tailored sapphire shirt, the very sight of him makes my mouth water.

I take a deep breath. Now or never. "Looking for me?"

Slowly, he turns around and smiles. "Of course, I am looking for you." He stands up and walks up to me. "I'm always looking for you." I notice the expression on his face as he searches mine. "Something is wrong. You are upset about something."

Tears well in my eyes as I think about our future, or possibly lack thereof. How did I get here? All the things I wanted were finally falling into place, and now I have to drop a bomb. "Can we have a minute to talk? There is something I need to tell you."

He moves in, closing the gap between us. I can see the unease in his eyes. His one look says so much.

Before he does anything to dissuade me, I open my mouth. "Conner, I think it's time to explain what happened the day you came looking for me after the incident at the amusement park. You destroyed something that was meant to be so beautiful and meaningful to us for the sake of your friends." He frowns and nods, then guides me to the couch where we both sit down. "That day. That day you stood by and participated in...," I inhale deeply. Tears stream down my cheeks. "That day you turned what was beautiful and meaningful to me, I would hope to you... Conner, I went home to end it. I wanted to kill myself. I wanted to die. I was done with life. I was upset because, at that moment, I got it. The realization hit me— I would never be who you wanted, someone who you could be proud of. You valued popularity more than me, and I was a fool to believe I could be enough." I continued to tell him the story on how my mom found me and how she sent me away for help.

He reaches for my hand. Fear stirs in his sad eyes. He changes from a man with confidence to a boy, pleading for acceptance in the blink of an eye. "I had no idea. I came to your house to apologize. To make it right. I was done with all the secrets that kept you and I apart. I wanted you no matter what. No matter who saw us or said anything. I wanted you. It was always you."

I grasp for courage. I'm not afraid of anything. I stiffen, pushing my shoulders back confidently. "But you always said, I want you Serena. It's you and me Serena. I don't care Serena. That's what you would say and I would believe you. But then you did what you did."

Conner shoots up of the sofa and begins pacing the room. "How long are you going to punish me for something that happened ten years ago? I tried to show you over and over again how sorry I am. I can't deal with this. I love you, but I can't stand by and have the old wounds reopen and fester. We're adults, and we should be able to move forward."

"Forward? Forward! You want ME to move forward." I jump up and cross my arms, gaping at him. I don't know what to say. All my life, I have worked hard to keep my sanity. To keep my old, insecure self at bay. "What do you want me to say? Wow, Conner, you fucked me up at seventeen, and now, at twenty-seven, I will forget all of the crap? Every tear I shed over you and your cowardice. I didn't know whether I was coming or going, or if I was ever going to make it over that hump. My mind was so screwed up, I thought whatever you threw at me was ok. You know what I see?" I wipe the tears streaming down my face. I'm trying to hold it together.

Conner stops and faces me, his mouth open and eyes wide as if I'd just kicked him in the gut. He has never seen me this angry at him. I always took what he gave me with a smile. I stand in my own two feet now. If he walks away, it would hurt and I would cry, but I would live. "What are we doing here? This is not what should be happening. I lived with this for ten years. I blamed you, blamed me, blamed the situation."

Conner scrubs his hand over his face and exhales. "Look you are getting ready to leave for the show. Maybe we need to look at this as a time to take a break. Things have moved quickly between us, and some space would do us good. I promise I won't be looking for anyone else. It will still be us, if you want it to be."

"Ok. We will take time and consider whether we want this or not?" I sigh, "I can agree to that."

He takes two strides and places his forehead against mine.

I pull away. "We will come back from this? Right?"

"I don't know, Serena. I don't know."

Chapter 24

Conner

I leave Serena's. Now that the dust has settled, I realize I let something significant to Serena be diminished by my own selfishness and insecurities. I caused her pain. So much pain that I could have lost her. Permanently, I keep running it through my mind, what if her mother didn't arrive? What if I stood up to my so-called friends? What if I was honest with myself? What if? What if? What if? Well, we wouldn't be in this position.

I walk down the street to the coffee shop. Angry sky matches how I feel. I look up and sigh. "What do I need to do?"

I love her. I don't know how to prove to her that we belong together. I will give her the time she wants and stay away. I won't be able to stay away for too long, though. For now, I'll have to support this adventure for her from afar. She needs to know I have her back.

I pluck my phone from my pocket and call Sally but, Ivan's deep timbre answers, "Hello?"

A mildly shocked and amused chuckle escapes me. "You don't sound like Sally."

"Sally is on my phone talking to Serena. She called for my advice on reality tv. Sal heard Serena through the phone and snatched it from my hand. They've been chattering like teenage girls ever since."

"So, what's up with you two? I thought you and Sally couldn't stand each other."

"Right now, we are getting along and hanging out. After you get over the bullshit, she really is a great girl. So why are you calling Sally? Are you looking to do something special for Serena on her last night in town?"

I glance down at my feet, hating the situation. "No" I huff, "I wanted to tell Sally to keep an eye on Serena." I hear her angrily shouting in the distance. Sally must have found out what happened.

"I'm going to kill him." I pull the phone away from ear and cringe. "That insensitive fuck. I can't believe I went to bat for him. Wait, Serena, Ivan is talking to someone on my cell. Ivan? Who is on my phone?" I hear my name in a hushed whisper. "Oh, HELL NO! How dare he call me! I am not speaking to him. I told him he needed to be cautious with her. She spills her soul to him, and this is how he repays her. Repays her by treating her like garbage. Give me that."

Scuffling noises fill up my earpiece, then Sally's voice rings clear as a bell. "Conner, we both know you made a big mistake by calling me. She's fragile and, just like on that day, she's out of it." She's out of it? Did I send her over the edge again? I can't do that to her again. I promised to never hurt her again.

I hear a disconnect and look at the screen. The dead space assures me that Sally's hung up on me.

My feet lug me up the street. My heart cracks under the weight of losing my best friend. Of losing my Serena. I drag myself up two flights of stairs to the small apartment I share with my friend, Gerry, from high school.

I never brought Serena here since he was one of the people who caused her so much pain. He thinks my infatuation with her began at the reunion. He has no idea. Why I kept it quiet all these years, I have no clue.

Maybe I am still afraid of people getting the wrong idea. My parents would have loved the idea for the wrong reasons. Serena's parents were influential in the community and my association would have given them a much-desired lift up. My friends, on the other hand, would have thought it social suicide. No friends would have accepted us as a couple and we would have crashed and burned.

"Dude, you look like you have gone ten rounds with Tyson. Did you have a fight?"

"Yeah, Serena and I are taking a break." I am resigned to the fact she and I are currently no more. I feel like a heartbroken teenager, waiting for my life to cease. This isn't the first time I've felt this way. I was hoping to never feel this way when it came to her again. If she would just wake up and realize these feelings, I have for her are real.

"So, you and the former fatty are no more?"

I grab him and fist his collar, slamming him into the nearest wall. I hoist him off the floor in a smooth motion. I am done with this crap. Joking or not, I'm tired of hiding. I am ripping at the seams with anger. He has no idea who she really is to me.

"Don't EVER talk about her like that. She is better than anyone. Serena is fucking better than you. Fat or not. I know I don't deserve her, but I will get her back. If I were you, I would turn your ass around and leave me be." I release my hold on him, step back, and clench my jaw. The urge to punch him builds in my fists, but I hold back. I need to work on this. I can't let her go. I don't want anyone else.

Chapter 25

Serena

It's the first week on the show, so the producers have us to choose from a list of songs for our performances. When the I spot my favorite Sugarland song on the list, Mitch turns to me and said, "You know this one." He pointed to the song on the list and smirked. He directed his next comments toward the musical director. "We are going with this."

I beam at him. My body vibrates with happiness. I got this. It's a sign. Maybe Mitch has changed. He seems so attentive and caring. My intuition may have been wrong about him.

Later we meet with the producers again. They want to talk about our image.

Producer Pete takes my hand and guides me to the stylist. "Ok, you are in desperate need of a makeover. This is Paulo. He will sculpt and design you into what our viewers will love."

My hand is placed in Paulo's hand. He drops a kiss on both of my cheeks, and I cringe. He seems fake and a little too eager to change me. For once in my life, I have no desire to change who I am.

"I see you are apprehensive. He is going to enhance, not change you." The producer ensures me before leaving the room.

Paulo presses his fingers together and touches them to his mouth. He squints at me, pursing his lips out against his fingers as he walked in a slow circle around me. "I see longer hair. I see smoky eye. Rock meets country. Outlaw style." His eyes widen, and he makes one loud, excited clap as if the light-bulb lit up in his head. "I got it—Miranda Lambert." Crossing my arms, I huff into the air in protest. Standing my ground, I decide to be firm in my changes. I change for nobody but me. "I want to look like me, not Miranda Lambert."

"You will be you; an updated version. I am not trying to make you a carbon copy. I am trying to design what the voters will love. Give it a try."

I bite my lip, knowing I'm about to change everything about me for votes; to stay in a competition; to promote myself and Mitch in this competition for popularity. Popularity. The one thing I always wanted. The one thing I have worked hard for. I want the popularity as me and not as anyone else's image of me.

I rub the back of my neck and pull on my chain. My Star of David charm swings back and forth with my nervous energy. I close my eyes silently whispering a mantra to myself. I take a deep breath and say the words that will be my ultimate downfall. "I'll do it."

The ever-popular host, Grayson Twist, speaks to the camera. His hair is perfectly coiffed and heavily gelled, tie perfectly knotted to match with his grey pinstriped suit. My body shakes, and my hands are suddenly wet. I stand there petrified.

Twist's slightly southern twang booms over the speakers. "Introducing them for the first time... Here are Serena and Mitch singing Sugarland's Baby Girl."

I have my in-ear monitors on as I approach the stage. I hear "test, one, two" in the earpiece. Though I have a calm and collected smile on my face, my hands are trembling. I scan over the cameras, lights and audience like a deer caught in headlights.

Once this finishes, maybe, just maybe, I will be able to breathe. The amazing craft service did wonders in comforting me this morning, bringing me anything I asked for—hot tea, magazines, and playing cards to keep my mind preoccupied. The downside of that was having to rein in my stress-eating habits. It's too easy to order all the tempting foods I crave during times like this.

All of the rehearsals, makeovers, and interviews have led to this moment. Now, I am in the hands of the public and their voting. I can't believe I am setting myself up to be judged again. The spotlight is on Mitch and I. Cameras appear to float down from the ceiling like nosey clouds and hone in on us. I take a deep breath.

Mitch says, "Ready?"

I feel like I am about to vomit. The video package of our introduction plays above us. I try to ignore it because I know they are doing a general history of both of us and our journey. My ears pique at some of the audience members' gasping while others blurt out nasty comments. Glancing over at Mitch, my lip starts to tremble and tears sting my eyes.

Mitch offers me an encouraging smile and opens his mouth to say something, but the announcer interrupts him. We are suddenly bathed in bright stage lights. The band picks up their cue and begins the song. I block everything and everyone out. I imagine I am at home singing in the bar; my happy place firmly in my mind, I inhale and sing.

I start at the mic stand as we rehearsed. It's hard to follow the band with these things in my ears. It's hard to concentrate. I pull one out of my ear and immediately feel more comfortable. I smile at Mitch and saunter over with the mic. I am in the groove, bouncing up and down, singing the end of the song with fervor. My smile is wide, knowing I finished strong and didn't lose my lunch.

Instantly, I wish Conner was here to see this. The fight pushed us back to the beginning, don't pass go, don't collect $200, just start all over again. I sigh and turn my focus to the judges.

They take their turns critiquing. First up Is Brett. He's all smiles, happy in his choice to move us to this spot.

The next judge is music producer Sylvia Chastain. Sylvia is well-known in the music world and is considered royalty and wears the regal air well. This woman can make or break a future with the smallest of sentences. And she is also in our corner.

The last judge on the panel is the famous hip-hop star, Triumph Butler. He's notorious for mixing popular music styles while adding his own flair. He isn't afraid to blend hip-hop with country or classical. He is considered a musical genius; a musical genius who wants to see us move on!

Everything is a complete blur. Comments are lost on me as I struggle to keep my composure. They liked everything-from our look, to the song choice, to my voice. The knowing glances over Mitch and I say more than I expected.

I beam. I look to Mitch on my left. Who would have thought he, of all people, would get me here?

The judges announce that if we go home, it will be a shock. I can't believe my ears. Did they really say that about me?

Chapter 26

Conner

I sit in my living room watching the show with my phone in hand, ready to vote. How could I not? I still love her and want her to be happy. I want her with me, but I'm sure I've ruined my chance. If only I had been patient and listened to what she said, not taken it personally that she hid her near suicide from me. She was brave to share her dark secret with me.

The introduction video begins, and I smile when I see her on the screen. They play a brief story of her life and how she got to this point. Serena looks great, not nervous at all.

I wait for our history to be broadcasted after the bullying is mentioned and childhood pictures appear on the screen. But they don't delve into it. I wonder if it will be revealed another week.

Pictures of Mitch and Serena together scroll across my screen. History of their personal and professional relationship appear before me, and I see red until she begins to sing. I watch her in awe. The camera loves her, but only I could see a little less sparkle in her eyes.

Mitch sidles up closer to her, wrapping one arm around her, and I would swear he is giving the camera a devilish smile. That smile is directed to me, I feel it in my bones. He is using this to his advantage. I want to jump through the tv and pull him off of her. I curse under my breath then I take a swig of beer. Gerry walks into the room, looks at the TV, and then at me. Ever since I told him about my true feelings for Serena, he seems to have left the past alone.

"Looks like someone is making a play for Serena."

I roll my eyes at him. "What are you trying to do? Pick yet another fight with me? Watch it, or I may give you a repeat performance of the other day." I am tired of fighting. I study the screen closely and see the smile on her face, I need us to get back to each other, but I have no idea how to get there.

The number I've been waiting for finally pops onto the screen. I call over and over again, stabbing the Call End button each time I hear the busy tone.

I relax my eager grip on my phone and sigh. She needs this, I know, but it's so hard being away from her. I concede to the distance tugging at my heart, knowing we'll be together when the time is right.

"I don't want to fight, but you may want to consider a shower, a shave, or at least trimming your beard. You look like you haven't left here in days. You are starting to look worse than the homeless guy on Eighth." He plops down on the chair across from me and continues. "It won't do you, or Serena, any good if she sees you looking like you've lost your damn marbles, man."

It's as close to an apology as I'll get from my old friend. "I don't want to admit you're right, but you are." I gulp the last of my beer, switch the tv off, and head for the bathroom. I refuse to let her see me fall apart like this.

Serena

Why is there a knock at my hotel room? And at this hour? I walk over to the door calling, "Who is it?"

"Me. Mitch. Let me in please?" What does he want?

I open the door and find him looking as sad and lonely as I am.

"Are you busy? Do you want to take a walk with me? Reminisce about old times? There's a cool bar down the street."

Why not? I've got nothing else going on. A drink couldn't hurt. "Sure, let me get my shoes on and grab my purse."

"Maybe you would like to change? I don't think pajamas are in style for drinks at Bar 24."

I glance down at my pajama bottoms and realize he is right. "Guess they won't let us in with me wearing rubber duckies." I walk over to the door to let him out. "Give me five- minutes."

He instead brushes by me and takes a seat in the chair next to the door before crossing his right leg over his left, making himself comfortable.

"Mitch, a little privacy please?"

He crosses his arms. "I am only waiting here to make sure you come. Sitting in this room moping is going to get you nowhere. Besides, I have an ulterior motive."

"And that is…" Like I didn't know already.

"We are both single." He uncrosses his leg and gets on the floor, sinking to his knees, begging. "Give me another chance, please. We owe it to each other to try."

The groveling sends my heart racing. I guess I will give it a try. "Let me change and we can talk. I don't want to ruin this working relationship. Just think about that for a few minutes."

I ransack the drawers to find some jeans and a tight-fighting tee, before making a beeline into the bathroom. I suppose I should treat this like a date. I take my time dressing and put extra care into my hair and makeup. Spritzing on a little perfume makes me feel sexy, and I also add a pair of silver hoops into my ears. Mitch always liked when I wore these hoops. When I wear my hair up, they accentuate my neck. Decision made; I pull my hair up into a ponytail.

"Ready to go?" I ask through the door as I open it.

I step through the doorway and watch his mouth gape and, eyes wide. "Something wrong Mitch?"

"No. Nothing is wrong. You look beautiful. You ready to go?" He extends his hand out to me and walks me to the door. "Let's have some fun tonight."

We exit the hotel and walk down to the end of the street. Then turn right to see the sign Bar 24 over the door. There is no line outside thank goodness, I just want to get in and sit at the bar.

We show our ids and are allowed in. I head toward the bar, but Mitch places his hand on the small of back and ushers me to a booth in the back corner. I feel nothing. No zing, no butterflies, nothing. It's nothing like when Conner touches me. My heart drops.

I slide my butt along the red leather booth and turn to put my feet up. It keeps Mitch from sitting on my side, so he slides into the other side.

A waitress approaches and he orders a beer. I can't decide so I stick with my old standby, a vodka with cranberry juice.

"How do you think we are doing on the show?" Mitch blurts out.

"I think we are going in the right direction. The idea is to stay out of the bottom two each week." The waitress delivers our beverages and I take a sip.

Mitch leans across the table and whispers in my ear, "Do you remember we used to have great rhythm together?"

I nearly spit out my drink. "Excuse me?"

I don't have the sparks with him. "Yes, I remember. I also remember how you found your rhythm with someone else."

I shouldn't be doing this. I shouldn't be leading him on. I don't want this. My heart belongs with Conner.

"Mitch, while I appreciate this time together, I am not feeling anything." He looks over to me and looks perplexed. "My heart is still with Conner."

"I get it. Sorry a guy can't try huh?" Mitch looks over and cheeks begin to redden from embarrassment.

Chapter 27

Serena

Sitting in the producer's office, I pick at the hem of my shirt.

We have been advancing week after week. Which makes me happy, but I'm also upset at the lack of control. There's no time to exercise between the rehearsals, photo shoots and appearances. My anxiety leads to stress eating. My clothes are fitting tighter. My face seems fuller when I look in the mirror. Stories from showbiz friends have proven that being called to the producer's office, only means one thing.

"Serena," he starts, "there has been a meeting to discuss some of the contestants and their changing appearances. There have been polls done on the show, and the viewers are suggesting you look heavier than normal. We know how the camera adds ten pounds. We need you to consider your health and try to work in a workout or two. Also, maybe you need to watch what you are eating from the craft service table. We are happy to place you with a nutritionist if you feel comfortable."

Tears stream down my face. I can't hide my utter shock, and embarrassment. Here we go again. It's probably only a matter of time before the jokes begin again. My mind races at the thought. "If I choose against it, what happens next? Are we fired from the show?"

"I wouldn't say fired. This is a reality competition show. I just wouldn't be surprised if you are voted off sooner than later. The public can be fickle. Take a little time and tell me your thoughts on this matter. In the meantime, I took the liberty to put workout time on the schedule for you." He checks his watch then smiles and nods politely before leaving the room. I clutch the bottom of my shirt, crying alone.

I'm shocked, but I know what I need to do. It's just so hard to hear it from the higher-ups. I wish I could stand up to them and say, "Hey I'm pretty too, just the way I am," but what is the use? I am fully aware I need to make it through to the final four at least. Then, if a record company is interested, I shouldn't have to worry as much.

I walk down the hallway and run smack dab into Mitch. "What did they say?" Mitch's question has a bite to it that I wish would abate, but his anger is well-placed after the other night.

"That, I need to consider my health if I want us to advance further in competition." I rub my eyes with the back of my sleeve gaining composure.

"You are listening to them, right?" He gingerly moves a strand of hair behind my ear. I look up at him hoping for something else to come out of his mouth anything but this. "I mean, if we don't have the right image, the public can vote us off."

My head snaps up and I roll my eyes. How shallow is he? This man has no clue. "We don't need to change; we are great just the way we are. Our talent should speak for itself."

"It appears the producers can change the outcome at any time. The voters like how we look together. We need to sell them on our image."

I am dumbfounded by all of this. I heard reality shows can do things to twist their outcome and change the emotional well-being of a contestant. They do it all the time on those dating shows.

Mitch frowns as I shake my head and make my escape to my hotel.

I call Sally for some reassurance, and tell her everything that transpired in the meeting.

"What does Mitch say?"

"Mitch says we, meaning I, need to work on this so we can move further and present a good image."

"That really sucks, Serena. I wish I could tell you to chuck the whole thing, but this is a great opportunity." She changes the topic. "So, what are you singing this week?"

"Well, it's eighties week, so I was thinking "No more words" by Berlin or "Only the Lonely" by the Motels."

"Both excellent choices, but "Only the Lonely" would show a slower side to your singing. Keep going, Serena. Keep your eye on the prize. Don't worry what these producers think. If the audience is with you and voting, it shouldn't be an issue."

"I know you're right. I love you."

"Love you too. Stay strong, because you are amazing."

I smile through a trickle of tears, wiping the droplets from my cheek. I don't know how strong I can be.

I decide to head to a bookstore to find some inspiration for writing. When I walk in, I notice a small, wire rack with magazines fanned across the shelves. My face stares back at me from under headlines like "She's in a downward spiral" to "From Fat to Thin to Fat Again." My eyebrows shoot up, and my throat tightens. There are articles focused on me and Mitch dating, on how I need to lose weight, and on why my old boyfriend really dumped me.

I can't believe I put myself in a vulnerable position again. I really need thicker skin. I can't be sensitive to this. I asked for the spotlight and, well, now here it is. My eyes rake over each picture and horrible headline until it reaches a cover that breaks my heart.

"Serena's Ex Moves On."

Beneath the bold print is a picture of Conner kissing another woman next to a photo of me. I grab the magazine off the rack and page through to the article. It suggests he left me because I had been gaining weight before the show even began.

My eyes fly over the page three times, devouring every nasty accusation. One a supposed quote from the new flame expressing her worry that Mitch might leave me too since I can't get my eating under control. I don't know what to think. My chest aches. My heart is destroyed.

Here we go again; my life on display with the court of public opinion. I thought we have been trying to work things out, but I see I'm going to have to call him. I still love him and seeing this garbage makes my blood boil.

The next show is only a few days away, and I have to focus. I can't though if I'm thinking about Conner with another woman.

I bite the bullet, pull my cell from my purse, and make a call with my heart lodged in my throat.

"Serena, is it you? Please don't hang up. We need to talk."

I take a deep breath. "What happened Conner? I saw you on the cover of a rag kissing another girl? How? Why? I thought we were on a break but not seeing anyone."

"We are, Serena, Look at the picture. Look at my arm. My tattoo is not there. I was photo shopped in with that girl."

I study the picture again. I don't see a tattoo. My fast breaths start to slow down.

"Serena, when are you going to let me back into that heart of yours? I need to be with you. To hold your hand and be in the audience cheering. I have been cheering from my fucking couch. I won't do it anymore. I am on the next plane out. I need to see you. Am I still yours or is the spin on the show about you and Mitch true?"

My eyes sting, and my voice is scratchy around a reply. "Yes, Conner. You are still mine. There's nothing happening with Mitch and me. But, have you seen me lately? I'm blowing up. Even the producers told me I need to lose weight."

"I want you, Serena. Fat, thin, curvy or bean pole. I love the inside of you. Your whole package. Your loving heart."

I put the magazine I was clenching back on the rack and bite back the flood of tears blooming from his words.

"For you to even give me a second chance, to even give it a try after how I treated you ten years ago...," he sputtered. "You, Serena, you are my true North. What I drove you to...I don't have the words to make you understand how sorry I am."

I tuck my arm around my middle, hoping to guard myself from any pain I might endure from giving into him.

"Serena, please. I'm begging here. Don't make me wait. What do you say?"

I follow my heart and take a deep breath. I am about to fall down the rabbit hole again. I sigh with my resolve. "When can you get here?"

Chapter 28

Conner

It is agonizing. Time creeps slowly, seemingly moving at a glacial speed.

I need to get to Serena as fast I can. I wasn't there during the first fallout. Actually, I was the one who created it so many years ago. The next flight available is in eight hours, and I plan to be on it. I call and book my seat.

I miss her. I miss the way she giggles when I kiss a certain area of her neck. Or how she melts when I kiss the back of her hand. I miss her hand caressing my face when we kiss.

Just the thought of her giving me another chance is makes me want to drive all night to get to her. I need to prove to her that my feelings are real and there are no ulterior motives her. I'm not a fame seeker or striving for a popularity status. After I lost her ten years ago, I made a vow I wouldn't let outside influences cloud my better judgment again. I will not let myself falter.

I attempt to pass the time with chores around the apartment, but nothing holds my focus so I grab the closest bag and stuff what I need inside. If I forget something, fuck it. I'm leaving for NYC, not a third world country. Sitting at the airport will be better than this.

I place a call to the cab company and order a cab.

It takes very little time for the cab to arrive. A honk of a horn, and I am looking outside my window to find the yellow and black checkered car with Next Big Thing advertised on the roof.

I exit the building and walk to the waiting car at the curb. Placing my bag on the sidewalk I open the door. I'm so scatterbrained I almost forget my bag sitting on the curb.

The airport is a welcome rush of activity as I wait in a painstaking long line to pass security. My mind is so fixed on the task at hand I forget to remove my watch and change. They have me go through the metal detector a couple times, resulting in me being pulled out of line by TSA to be checked and searched further.

"Mr. Fortenberry can you step this way with me, please?"

All I keep thinking to myself is you've got to be kidding me. I have to catch this flight. I want enough time to grab a coffee and get to my gate. At this point there will be no coffee for me. I need caffeine when I cross paths with Mitch.

"Yes, sir. What seems to be the problem?" I look at his badge. "Officer Smyth."

"A precaution I need you to step inside here while I pat you down and search you further."

This is ridiculous, but I cooperate and follow.

It seems to take forever.

Checking my watch, I see that my leisurely walk through the airport is gone. Now I'm lucky to have enough time to get the coffee I'll need in case I run into Mitch. I grab my coffee and make it to the gate just in time and pass over my ticket to the agent. With a smile, she ushers me down the small walkway, to enter the plane. I look at the row numbers, while people staring at me. The plane is rather small, it's only two seats on either side. Before placing my bag in the overhead bin, I grab my phone and tap off a quick text to Serena to let her know I am on my way. I turn the phone off and buckle in.

The plane taxies to the runway and I take a deep breath as we lift off. Once we are in the air, I release it and start fidgeting in my seat. The person sitting next to the window stares at me.

"Are you alright?" the kind older gentleman asks.

I force my leg to stop bouncing and look over at him. "Yeah, I'm ok. Just nervous. I hate flying. I'm on my way to see my girlfriend. We've been apart for a little while, and I haven't seen her in weeks. I'm nervous as to how she will react when she sees me. When she left, we didn't end it but we didn't say we would stay together. I love her." I can't stop opening up to this complete stranger. Why do I feel like I can tell him anything?

"Listen son, I don't know what happened or why, but you seem to know what you want. If you love her, you're doing the right thing. I would have chased my Betsy to the ends of the Earth." He removes a handkerchief and stares at it lost in thought. "She was my everything." He smiles but it doesn't meet his eyes. He turns away and stares out of the window. I get the feeling he doesn't want to talk anymore so I look down at my watch. I countdown the minutes till we land.

The plane lands, and I grab the first taxi to the hotel. I got a room where Serena was staying thankfully. I want to make sure she knows I'm not forcing her into staying with me, but that she matters enough for me to stay nearby.

I stand in front of the large bay window looking out over the city skyscape. She's here. I'm not sure exactly where, but I feel the magnetism between us grow stronger as I travel closer.

The show blocks their rooms on the top two floors, requiring special access to the rooms. I hate being so close yet so far away.

I send her a text letting her know I've arrived the moment I pulled up to this swanky hotel in the heart of New York, but still no response.

To keep myself busy, I grab the remote and turn on the TV, but I'm flipping through tv channels I'm not even paying any attention to does little to soothe my restlessness.

I assume she's in rehearsal, mentoring or the studio. She must be loving the studio time. I scroll through my phone and search for the music library that has the playlist of the songs she has sung on the show so far. I bought each one as soon as it became available. Pressing play for the first song, my heart warms. I love listening to her sing and it makes me feel like she's with me.

Fuck, it is as if I'm whipped. But I don't care. Maybe I am. Maybe this will end up being a solo venture, but I know I will never find anyone like her. Call her my soulmate, the seal on my fate, I don't care. I know I will never love another like her, reciprocated or not.

I hoist my suitcase onto the bed, begin unpacking, and wait to hear from Serena. A knock jars me from my thoughts. Pulling open the door, I'm greeted by one of the show's producers holding a stack of papers in his hand. A cameraman stands behind him, lugging a professional-grade camera on his shoulder.

"Hello, my name is George, and I am with the show. Before you can see Serena, I need you to sign some forms." He passes me the documents.

I have no idea what I am looking at. It looks like a simple press release. I go ahead and sign the form. Anything for Serena.

He continues, "May we come in and do a small interview with you that will run in this week's package for the show? Just a few questions to help our viewers understand Serena better through the time of your outward public shaming."

I cringe hearing the phrasing. I guess it's time to tell.

George's petite blonde assistant carries in two folding chairs and stages them in a section of the room with the best light. The cameraman clips a mic to my shirt the directs me to sit in one of the chairs. George sits across from me with a list of questions. "So, Conner, tell us what Serena was like back then. She seems to have been larger than life."

"Serena has always had a great heart, and, yes, she was then and still is larger than life. Her smile is contagious. Though my past self would have been perceived one way around others. When no one was watching, she was mine. I hate my part in her unfortunate past. I wish I was a stronger person for her, for myself."

"Which leads to the next question. When you saw her after all these years, what were you feeling?

Hoping for?"

"I was apprehensive, but hopeful. I followed her life through her ups and downs, quietly behind the scenes, acquiring information from her friends." I glance out the window for a moment, recalling how much I wanted to be with her even then, and shrug. "I loved her from a distance I always wished God made me different; - strong, so I could handle the backlash from people whose opinions shouldn't have mattered."

"So, tell us some things you would call Serena in public."

I hesitate, ashamed of the things I said about her years ago. "You name it, we said it." I shift uncomfortably in my chair. I don't want to relive this mess. I'm trying to get her back not push her further away. "Fatty, ugly, chunky monkey, wide load, chubby." I drop my gaze to my hands, fiddling with the last button on my shirt. It's so uncomfortable to admit this out loud, to confess the terrible acts of a time long past. "This one kid put tacks on her seat to see if she would pop if she sat on it. We were very cruel. How she made it through I don't know."

"How would you feel if Serena gained weight back?"

"I would care for her no matter what..." He cuts me off mid answer. This line of questioning sends red flags flying in my head.

"Does Serena know you are here?"

Unease creeps up my spine. I know shows can twist and manipulate my words. I need to end this now! Rising from my chair, I walk toward the door to cue my intention of ending the interrogation. "If you're done, I need to take care of some personal business."

George smirks, stands to let his assistant gather the chairs. "I think we have everything. If we need anything else, we know where to find you." He winks at me, and they leave.

I close the door and consider how this might go down. Maybe the producers want to humanize her for more votes. Maybe he wants to show the poor judgmental side to get viewers to vote her off. Either way, if he messes up, I will have to fight a lot harder for us than I planned.

Chapter 29

Serena

I grab a bottled water from the drink cart and take a breather while the band hashes out the final details for this week's show. We are getting down to the final four, and I am more anxious than ever. Knowing Conner is waiting in the hotel somewhere sends my emotions into jumbled frenzy. I'm not sure how I feel about him being here. I want him with me, but I'm apprehensive. I think, after everything that went down, it is a good idea we separated from each other to protect ourselves.

The producers request an interview with Conner before I see him. They claim it is for the video package before our performance. I agree, but something doesn't feel right in my gut.

Aside from the stress with Conner, the show continues to scrutinize every pound I gain even though the audience's' support is stupendous. I'm trying everything I can to maintain my weight loss, but, in the end, stress is winning.

I find myself slinking back into my shell. I've caught myself walking with my head down more times than not, avoiding eye contact with other people. The former fat girl is winning. The more the producers complain, the more I stress. The more I stress, the more I revert to eating.

I walk toward the elevators and press the down button. I need to get to him and see his face, knowing when I see him I will be able to keep calm. He can assure me that everything will be fine.

When I knock at his door, I take a deep breath and say a silent prayer. I pray that things will go back to normal for us. Whatever normal is.

Conner opens the door, looking like I feel. Like we both went ten rounds in the ring. He seems so sad but beams at me like I am his oasis in the desert.

He speaks softly. "Hey Serena." His hand lifts to cup my cheek. Actual tears well in his eyes. "I am sorry. So sorry." His other hand raises, trapping my face in his palms. I relax under his touch and drink in his sincerity as he adds, "I should have been more understanding, more loving. I love you, and nothing will change that. I know I have a lot of making up to do."

I can't help it. I smile through tears of my own. "I am sorry too. I should have given you time to process and not expect you to understand right away..." I'm interrupted by firm hands dragging me into the room. He crushes my mouth with his. When he lets me go, I notice my swollen lips in the mirror behind him. "Wow. Who needs collagen? Just kiss you and bam, big lips..." I wander toward the center of his room, and his arms engulf me, hugging me tightly. I giggle, pushing on his chest. "Hey, a little air here, Conner. I can't breathe."

"I need to tell you some things so we are on the same page with my interview." Conner opens his mouth to add to the conversation, but a knock on the door stops him.

There is another wrap on the door. Conner opens the door and is followed back inside by George exclaiming, "Great, you're both here." The slimy douche is one person I can't stand the sight of. "I see in your schedule; we have time for a short interview together."

I roll my eyes, groaning with annoyance. He reaches around me for a side hug, and I recoil at his touch. I swear he's up to something. I put on a smile to appease him for sake of the band, but it's as fake as my nails and hair extensions.

"Our Serena here is the talk of the town these days. Have you seen all the news reports on her and Mitch doing well with the audience?"

He is such a liar. They may be supportive to the public, but behind closed doors, they treat me like a disease. I am starting to see a pattern here. How do I get into these situations?

I gently shrug George's arm off of my shoulder. "George, can we do this quickly? I haven't seen Conner in a couple of months, and I would really like to spend some time with him before rehearsals begin again."

"Sure thing. I'll bring in the cameraman and get you mic'd up."

Sweat beads on my forehead. I feel cold, clammy, and lightheaded. Maybe if I faint, we can get out of doing the interview.

Once we are seated, he dives right in. "We know some of the history between you two from previous video packages, and I must say it is a bizarre one. Serena, why would you let this continue throughout your senior year of school? Were you that desperate for a boyfriend? For someone to love you?"

"Excuse me," Conner shouts in response to George's prying. "Desperate? She wasn't desperate. How dare you?"

George nods his head, pretending to feel touched by Conner's reaction.

"Conner, relax. I will answer the question. It's easy for someone to think I was desperate, lonely, and eager. I can tell you though, George, the connection we had back then was different than any relationship I've had since."

"Conner, how do you feel about Serena performing with her ex? Has Mitch tried to make a play, Serena? How do you both feel about being separated with the tour coming up?"

Conner stiffens at my side, but doesn't reply, so I answer. "As far as I know, Conner was ok with it when I was approached to join his band."

"As for being separated," Conner interjects, "I feel we will be fine. I trust her, and she trusts me. If there is no trust... there is no love." Conner glances my way, grabs my hand and kisses it.

George clears his throat. "That's all well and good. What about the outside influences like the tabloids? Rumors can spread and wreak havoc on one's relationship. I know you have seen it all over. Once the seed is planted, doubt can grow," he says with a smug smile. "It is hard to keep a relationship together in this industry. Especially when the star is a woman. I mean, when the significant other is treated like a second-class citizen—"

"It's something we don't need to worry about there, George. I am happy for Serena. I LOVE her. I don't care if she is famous and I'm not. I never wanted the spotlight. I'm not a fame seeker. If all I am known for is being involved with Serena then I am okay with that. Don't feed your negativity to us."

George swallows hard and adjusts his tie. He's flustered. Good. He needs to hear how he feeds on us for ratings.

"Weren't you the fame seeker in your school? Isn't that why you shied away from admitting your 'relationship' to your friends, because you knew if that happened, your life, as you knew it, was over? I guess I don't quite understand the fascination. Did you get a high off of it? A thrill if it were?

Conner gets up, rips the mic off of his shirt and storms toward the door. "I believe you are done here, George. You've gotten all the history lesson I'm willing to give. Now, gather your things and get out, or you'll regret it."

Chapter 30

Serena

I remove my mic and walk toward the door. George and his cameraman take their equipment and disappear. Conner thrusts his arm out across my chest, blocking me from leaving as he shuts the door.

My brows shoot up, surprised by his action. "I... I thought I would go too. You don't need me here."

"You, my dear, are not going anywhere. We are alone, and I need to be near you. You don't have to be at the studio for a little while, and I have some lost time to make up for." He moves my hair to the side and kisses my neck. "This has to go." he says, plucking the neckline of my shirt. You seem to be way overdressed for what I want to do to you right now."

He leads me to the bed and kisses me with a need I have never seen from him before. Like I was his lifeline, and he needed me to breathe. He begins the slow, tantalizing dance of removing my clothes. First, my pale, pink gauzy tunic lands on the floor in a crumple mess. Next, he unbuttons my jeans and shimmies them down my hips.

"Wait!" I giggle, against his mouth, "My heels."

"I'll remove them if you let me put them back on. They are so sexy, and the idea of your heels digging into my ass while I take you turns me on." He waits for my answer, quirking a wicked smile.

I bite my lip, so distracted by the need he stirs in me that I'm not sure if I nodded my head.

He kneels down, slipping one patent-leather pump off, then the other. His fingers tuck into the top of my denim, and he drags my jeans down, the sweet friction heating my skin. After slipping my heels back on, Conner leans back on his feet and drinks me in. "A perfect sight, if I do say so myself."

My hot-as-hell heels always made me feel beautiful, but the way he looks at me as I stand in my camisole, panties, and cherry-red shoes makes me feel like a goddess.

I move to grab the hem of his shirt, intending on undressing him as soon as possible, but he steps back and shakes his head.

"Honey I want to show you how much I missed you first, then... I will get naked and show you again." He clasps my hand with his and pulls me to the bed. Patting the mattress, Conner gestures for me to sit. "Don't be shy Serena. Not now."

"Are you sure you want me? Look at me, I'm not looking my best, and I don't want you to be disappointed. I mean, you hear what they are saying in the media; I am blimping up. You don't want to be with someone in the spotlight, especially when it's in a negative way."

"How many times do I have to tell you? Serena, you are beautiful no matter what size. I am sorry that I ever made you doubt yourself. We were teenagers then, and I was stupid. If I could tell my younger self to not listen to the bullshit and just follow my heart I would." He eyed my reaction, continuing when I didn't protest his reminder of how different we are from those kids and how sorry he is now. "Now that is settled, I need to touch and taste you. To watch you come apart at my hands and mouth. You think we can continue?"

"Of course, we can."

He removes my camisole, gently peels my panties down my bared legs, and lay me down. Conner climbs onto the bed, straddling me. He kisses a path from my lips, to between my breasts, and down my stomach until his face hovers over my mound. He groans and lowers his head, grazing his nose in my crease. His sharp inhale sends shivers up my core. "Mmm. Someone is ready for me, aren't you, my love?" He sweetly traces my wet, sensitive lips with his tongue. I feel the sensation all the way down to my toes. "You taste like heaven. I could feast on you all night."

All I can manage is a pleasure-filled moan. He wants to take his time with me, but I am on a schedule. As if he can sense it, he whispers, "Don't worry I will make sure you get where you need to go in the next thirty minutes. Tonight, though, when filming is over, you are all mine." Those words made me weak in the knees. My core clenches. I hold on to him for dear life as he gives me a ride I won't forget.

Chapter 31

Serena

I wake with a start. The alarm is blaring, and my surroundings are unfamiliar. Surveying the small room, my brain decides to revive itself, and I suddenly remember I'm in Conner's room and not at the set. I squint at the numbers on my phone and realize it's time for my hair and makeup session.

After throwing my feet over the edge of Conner's bed, I coax them to work. Halfway jogging, halfway fumbling, I pull my clothes on and make a mad dash to my trailer on the east end of the studio lot next to the hotel.

"It's about damn time," Grace Kemp whines as she taps at her watch. She mulls over the various outfits spread out all over the seating area.

A knock on the door, followed by, "Make-up time, bitches," indicates that I need to leave Grace in my trailer and meet Nilsa in the room next door, which I like to call the beautification station.

I sit in the chair and consider the reflection my face presents in the mirror. I try to form a smile because of all that has happened in the last twenty- four hours, but the stage fright is taking over once again.

Minutes later, Nilsa and Stacia start their magic. My hair gets wrapped around huge rollers, and they smear cakey foundation on my face. That crap feels like a hundred pounds on my skin. Their hands work around each other so fluidly as they transform me, I can barely tell whose hands are where on my head. They fuss over what I'll look like on camera. The two-take picture after picture, changing details of my look here and there until they are happy with how the camera image appears. Picture after picture the click gives a sample of their work and what needs to be approved.

A swift knock pulls my attention toward the door. The stylist enters just as Nilsa sprays my hair for the twentieth—and hopefully the last—time. Clapping his hands, the stylist assesses my look. "Great! Loose waves with a couple of sections crimped will work with this ensemble."

A frown tugs at my lips. I hate my hair down, but apparently, it's what the outfit calls for. They dress me in acid wash jeans with the layered neon-colored tank tops. A wide black belt with a big silver buckle is fastened around my middle, and black spike-heeled boots finish off my ensemble.

I look like the eighties threw up on me. It's funny, the look is making a comeback.

I exit the beautification station and meet Mitch outside my trailer. He is wearing acid wash jeans as well, but he gets to wear a comfortable vintage Van Halen t-shirt instead of shirts so bright they give you a headache.

"Are we really wearing this?" he grumbles. "Why can't it be about the music, instead of how we dress?"

"I think we got off easy. Did you see what they are making Allegra wear? Cindy Lauper's doppelganger has arrived." I point to the pretty girl in the crinoline and neon-striped hair. She looks like the cover of She's So Unusual. She raises her hand to wave, but drops it when she notices that we are gawking at her crazy transformation.

I smile politely to help her feel less awkward. "Hey, Allegra, you ready for this evening?"

"More than ever. I love Cindy Lauper, and, hey," she ruffles her skirt and flails her arms out. "Girls just wanna have fun." Allegra's cheery expression saddens, and she huffs out a disheartened sigh. "Who am I kidding here? My hair looks like a My Little Pony took a shit on my head."

We all have a good laugh, and Mitch walks into the trailer. "So, have you been watching the entertainment news? I feel like I'm everywhere." Why can't they leave me alone? My voice should matter, not my history or who I'm dating."

Ever since Conner showed up, I have been able to breathe. I'm a little more relaxed and very happy—aside from my often-awkward encounters with Mitch. Every now and then, Mitch still flirts and thinks he's got another chance, but I shoot him down every time. I wish he would move on. Sometimes I catch the way the other girls in the competition look at him. He's got to see it too. I wish he would let them in. He might actually have fun.

Once we finish soundcheck, we move to the green room and hang out while the last preparations are made for filming. I want to eat, but I am afraid of people staring and judging me. Mitch motions for me to follow him to the food table. My face pales and my hands moisten.

"Come on Serena, let's go get something to eat."

My stomach growls at the suggestion, but a seed of panic blooms in my chest. "You know I can't," I mumble. "They are watching me." My hands start to tremble with the fear of what they'll think.

"Listen, you need to eat something, or you are going to pass out on stage. I don't want to lose votes because you pass out," Mitch reasons.

"I also don't want to lose any votes because I am too fat." I glare at him, annoyed.

He doesn't get it. He crooks an eyebrow at me and purses his lips, letting me know he'll make me eat, one way or another.

I concede and follow behind him, spooning food onto my plate. I sit in a corner chair, as far away from everyone as I can get, and push my food around with my fork, even though I want to eat it so badly.

"Serena?" One of the PA's holds an envelope out to me, yanking me from my food trance. I take it and offer a grateful nod. I'm shocked to see it's Conner's writing on the front. I flip open the letter and read silently.

Serena,

Break a leg tonight. I don't need to really say that because you will be great. I will be in the audience, watching and cheering you on. I love you, remember that.

Forever yours,
Conner

I send him a quick text message of thanks and wait to get my mic and pack attached.

As I watch show-hands buzz about the room, readying us contestants, chills run over my skin. An unexplainable unease waves through my body. I brush the agitation away and take the stage, waiting for the show to begin.

The announcer welcomes the viewers back to this week's episode and introduces the remaining contestants. Spotlight's hover over each singer or band before sweeping back to the host. When lights and cameras are focused back on him, I duck off the stage to wait my turn to perform in the third segment. During the first two performances, I jump up and down and pace the side stage to keep myself awake and energized. The host cues us to join him on stage once again, and this week's video package rolls for the viewers.

I scan the audience and find Conner near the middle. My smile widens until I notice his face fall. His voice chimes in on the screen behind me, and I turn to watch his interview with the rest of the world. It made me look desperate... needy. I can't help my tears fall as old pictures of me surfaced with his voiceover, talking about how fat I was. When he recalls some of the terrible nicknames, he and his friends called me, my stomach flops. I gaze up at the screen in disbelief, my insides churning from the bitter memories. I look like a deer in headlights...like a fool.

When the reel finishes, I run off stage. I lean against a wall out of the camera's sight and clutch my chest, heaving suffocating breaths in and out. Air. I can't get enough air. Flashbacks of the day in the amusement park weasel their way through my thoughts. Flashbacks of all the times I was bullied in public and loved in private.

The stage manager looks at me in annoyance and pushes me back on stage. I can't breathe. I am embarrassed. Attempting to pull myself together, I search the center aisles until I see Conner again. He stares back at me, his face twisted in a look of shock and regret.

Something in me snaps. My anger for Conner and having to rehash the past. My anger at the producers for pulling this stunt. They are trying to rile me up, but it won't work. I turn it all off. The emotions, the sadness, the memories, they were all gone and a fire lights within me. I reach for the mic with determination and glance at Mitch. He smiles, pride beaming from his eyes. He finally sees me fighting back.

Every note I sing tonight is to show I am somebody. My mind awakens. I'll show them, I think.

I sing the opening lines and direct them to Conner. I need to reassure him I am ok and what was said won't hurt me. Turning to Mitch, as a direction from the producers I sing to him while he plays guitar. My focus needs to shift. More of a connection they want.

Flirting. I am flirting.

I give a wink to the camera and strut to the other side of the stage. I shake and undulate to the high-pitched, melodic whine of the saxophone. I am on fire. The audience is hooting and hollering as if I am already a rock star. I haven't heard it this loud for us since week one. Sliding my gaze over the excited guests, I notice the pleased expressions on the judges' faces. They are even tapping their feet to our rhythm.

"Serena... Serena... Serena…" Sylvia stands along with the other judges and claps for a standing ovation. Once they sit back down, she proceeds. "Where did that come from? The voice, the attitude, the ease? You looked like you were comfortable up there," Sylvia says.

"First, are you alright?" Brett concern touches me.

I nod, yes, even though I am completely angry and terrified.

"What happened in the past was wrong, but it seems you have taken that negativity and channeled it into something amazing. You were on point. Well done!"

I didn't know how to respond except to smile.

Triumph stands and is applauding again. "I am surprised. Finally, this," he gestures to Mitch and me, "this takes me back to Serena of week one. Mitch, the guitar solo was fantastic, superb, a great take on an eighties classic. I can't wait to see what you have in store next week."

We walk off stage, and I'm more determined than ever to prove everyone wrong. I'm not done yet. I will rise back up and continue the path to winning. Serena is no one's loser.

Chapter 32

Serena

We make it through to next week by the skin of our teeth. The results showed us at the bottom of the leaderboard. Thankfully, we made it to a new week and a new theme. This week's theme is duets. The producers assigned us a specific artist's song collection, from which we pick a song to sing on the upcoming episode. I was given Terri Nunn. Not only are we going to sing her songs, but actually sing with her. The Terri Nunn from Berlin. My nerves get the better of me. My palms begin to sweat. I scan the rest of the songs and my eyes widen. There were too many songs on the list to choose from.

While everyone would expect me to choose the ballad Berlin made famous, Mitch and I chose my personal favorite, "The Metro." I continued down the list and saw the other song we must do. We chose her duet from the movie "Sing" as our second option. With the way last week went, I need a safety song.

I'm nervous the video package will hurt me. Luckily, I am wrong, and we're safe.

I don't know how I will react to meeting her. I think I might be tongue tied. Her songs were a part of the soundtrack of my life, and I hope she doesn't think I'm a complete stalker.

I sit in the rehearsal room, continuously tapping my foot on the footrest of the stool. We wait with bated breath, as she saunters in the room. My palms start to sweat, yet again, and my jaw aches from smiling so wide. I remember watching her music videos, VH1's Bands Reunited, and anything else that featured her and her music.

She extends her hand for a shake. "Ms. Nunn, I am so excited to meet you. I have been a fan since I was a kid. I can't believe I get to sing with you."

"I heard you picked The Metro?" The cameras are surrounding us to get our reactions. They watch our every move, hoping to get some sort of conflict. I hate to tell them… they won't find it here.

I nod. My mouth has gone too dry to talk.

"Well, it's a great song, and I can't wait to see what you two have come up with to split the song for a duet. In my opinion, alternating verses would be ideal, but I am willing to play around to find what works best. What I would like to do is hear you sing the song all the way through to see where I can pop in."

I nod again, take a swig of water, and begin my rendition of her lyrics. After finishing the song, she looks at me with awe. With bright eyes and a wide smile, she claps, slowly at first then faster and louder as she rises from her chair in a congratulatory cheer. "I don't know where I can jump in. I guess I can take the second verse." Teri gestures for the cameras to leave. Once they are out of sight, she continues. "You sound amazing. The strength, the power I hear is incredible. I am dumbfounded, and please don't take this the wrong way, but I wonder why they are giving you such a hard time."

"It's because I gained weight, and they want someone who's thin to win. I understand that, I guess, but I wish they based it on my talent rather than my looks."

"When this is all over, you will still get the mean ones looking at your appearance. But some will fall off and judge you by your talent first." She seems very concerned and knowledgeable about where I was coming from. "Don't let the light blind you until you can't see. Always let the ones who care and love you in."

I look at her and consider her words. In the genuine pride and knowledge of her expression, I see something I'd had a hard time accepting all my life, more so lately. I need to be me, my true, authentic self.

"Now that I have given you words of wisdom," she slung an arm around my neck, "we need to look at song number two. Luckily, I'm just coaching this one. This shit is going to be incredible. So… I don't have to sing it." She smiles, and we all share a laugh.

Rehearsal continues with ease until we leave the studio and are bombarded by flashing bulbs and people shouting questions. Can't they find someone else to pick on? Didn't the new bachelor pick his girl yet? This is one time I wish I could hide away from all of this, to be invisible again. Ah, the price of being in the spotlight of my own three ring circus.

I walk into my room, and the phone is ringing off the hook. I answer it, and the voice on the other line is the travel agent for the show. "Serena, I need to discuss with you and Mitch your travel plans for the hometown visit. The local affiliate has an event planned at your high school. The town wants to give you and Mitch the key to the city."

"They do realize that Mitch did not attend the same high school I went to. Nor did he live in Briar Glen, right?" I remind the travel agent from the show.

"Oh, the town is aware. They are treating this as mostly your day Serena. Enjoy it. Congratulations. Please stop by my office for your itinerary. You leave tomorrow morning. Before I hang up, she adds, "Will Conner be there as well? We need to make sure he is front and center. We would love for the two of you to walk through the halls and maybe talk about your history. We also want to see your parents and interview them. Oh, and if you have any friends living in the area, please invite them as well. We want to see the interaction and get the great sound bites about you and Mitch. Mitch will need to do the same. I know he lives in a different area, which is a distance, but they really want your story."

When she finally stops talking and lets me get a word in, I take a deep breath and nod. "Ok, we will be by later." I hope this doesn't create strife between Mitch and myself. We always thought we would be on equal footing. It appears this is not the case. They have placed me in the forefront. We never really discussed what we would do if this happened. I suddenly become nervous and afraid to make waves with Mitch.

After the debacle from the last show, Conner left. He wasn't leaving me in an emotional sense, but he wanted to remove himself from anymore issues that may cause more harm than good. The downside to his leaving is that I really need him right now.

I send a quick message to let him know I will be home tomorrow, and that I needed to go over what the head of travel said. My chest tightens thinking about taking the show to my hometown.

I call my parents, feeling a little guilty I haven't made time to talk with them more often. The schedule is daunting and calling is hard. I am relieved they aren't home. Though I missed them, I didn't feel like hashing out the low-lights of my experience on the show recently.

I leave a quick message. "Hey ma, it's me," like she doesn't know her own daughter's voice, "I am calling to tell you I will be arriving home tomorrow for the hometown visit. I won't need to be picked up from the airport. Mitch and I will have a car. Please be prepared. You and dad may be interviewed again. The mayor is giving me the key to the city. Producers are wanting me to walk them through the school. I think it's time you and Conner try to make amends and get along. I know we have had a rocky return, but I need your support on this. Please support me. Love you both." I hang up the phone, silently praying that everything goes well. I don't need another week of drama.

I call Ivan and then Sally; both tell me they will be there. I wonder if they are going to arrive together; I secretly hope so. He is leaving for LA soon to star in the troupe for Ballroom Blitz. Hopefully, he will move up the ranks quickly.

I pack my little carry-on bag and take a cleansing breath. I really hope all goes as planned with this visit. I really hope we can get through it.

Chapter 33

Serena

The flight is uneventful, but I still white-knuckle the seat all the way there. The notion of going back, and not of my own volition, terrifies me. Sitting between Mitch and one of the producers, I didn't know if voicing my fears will be helpful or harmful. These producers are enjoying grabbing every little nasty tidbit or secret to keep ratings afloat.

After deplaning, we are pushed in the direction of the exit. People are everywhere in the baggage claim with signs of welcome and pure fandom. Once again, the camera is there to capture all the footage.

A town car picks us up and whisks us to a hotel, where we're handed keys without waiting and ushered to our rooms so we can quickly change for interviews and the performance. I have makeup applied and hair touched up. They match a flowing scarf with my dark wash jeans, black boots and blue jeweled-colored sweater. I wrap it around my neck and leave my hair down. "Well, here goes nothing." I smile in the mirror.

I must be standing there a little too long because, the phone on the nightstand gets my attention. I slam the door and rush downstairs. The car, more like an SUV is waiting for me. Mitch is in there already tapping his watch. "A little late, are we?"

"Sorry. Need to be perfect." I'm freaked out and scared. No one needs to know it. The drive to the school has me on edge. The SUV windows are tinted blocking the outside from looking in. The air feels stagnant and I hyperventilate.

As we exit the SUV, I try to take deep breaths but that doesn't seem to calm my nerves. I look at all the people here to see us and it's overwhelming.

Mitch brought his guitar, so we could sing an acoustic set of three songs. I look into the audience and see Conner on the bleachers. Among the sea of fans, locals and just the plain curious, he's giving me a thumbs up. He looks at me with devotion, offering the love and support I need right now.

I approach the mic on the makeshift stage outside on the fifty-yard line and start with my favorite Sugarland song. Mitch and I look at each other beaming. He knows how important this is to me. We play off of each other. The crowd sets into a low rhythmic stomp on the bleachers in sync with us. The cameraman captures the crowd's excitement shot for shot. It is fun to see the people who despised me so long ago cheering for me like I was their best friend. I even spot one with a tee shirt that says, "Vote for Serena and Mitch."

We finish our short set and then the mayor offers up the key to the city, proclaiming it "Serena and Mitch Day." This is the vindication I am looking for. To be recognized for my accomplishments by the people who never really cared. Now, they have to care or at least pretend for the cameras. "We're ready," the PA came over with a flourish.

My elbow is grabbed and I'm forced in the direction of the building. I haven't stepped inside since the day I graduated. The blonde at my elbow keeps pushing me forward and rambling on.

"You will now give us a tour of the school. You know show us your old locker, favorite class, favorite teacher…"

We walk down the main hallway of the school. I feel anxious looking at some of the pictures of each class. In a glass display case, I focus on a picture surrounded by trophies and medals. The group in the gold frame is my class, ten years younger and a whole lot naiver.

The show's designated traveling interviewer notices me staring at the picture and must realize that I'd found a piece of my history.

"Okay, Serena, that's great…stand right there, but turn a little toward your left," the thin, perky blonde directs. "You got a good shot of that, Sam?" The cameraman nods. "Tell me, Serena, how does it feel being back in your old stomping grounds?" The blonde shoves a mic up to my mouth and waits for an answer with a fake smile plastered on her face. I answer, though they already know my answers. I peer beyond the camera to Conner who stands in Sam's shadow, his calm expression encouraging me to push through the rehashing of bad memories.

In my periphery, I see my mom glaring at Conner. He keeps his eyes trained on me, though, like nothing else matters. It is at that moment; Mitch decides to grab my hand. I think he did it as a friendly gesture at first, but when I see the daggers, his gaze is shooting at Conner, I know it is something different. When the interviewer ends the session of our jog down memory lane, I meet Conner's shocked gaze and shake my head once, hoping he senses I am just as shocked as he is.

We walk into the auditorium. The local news has set up time to question us during the show's walk-through, and this is where they've set up. We are ushered to a line of director chairs that form a semi-circle in the center of the stage floor.

They ask to interview my parents first. I'm petrified. I have no idea what my parents will say. Sometimes they have absolutely no filter. I make sure to appear ecstatic on the outside, but on the inside? Well? Let's say I am holding my breath. Mom starts, "Well, Serena was always a musical child. She also had such a flair for the dramatics."

I cringe at the last comment.

Dad interjects "I remember, when she was three years old, she would stand in front of the house and sing for all the neighbors. You could ask her to sing anything from a tv theme song to a soda jingle. She didn't care. She always did it with a smile on her face." I sink in my chair with embarrassment. "It was when she pursued her talents in high school that we knew she was really going somewhere." He puts his hand on mine and gives me a gentle smile.

I shift in my seat, dreading the next part of the interrogation. I know the next round of questions will have to do with what I endured in school. I hate to relive this over and over again. What more can be said? Yes, I was a fat, obese, whatever you want to call it, as a child. Yes, I let my need for friendship and attention from the opposite sex cloud my judgement on the dating scene. Yes, I should have stood up for myself more and not hid behind my books and extracurricular activities.

"Serena, take us back to the moments you found yourself being bullied. We have received many emails and letters of praise for your triumph on the show. The public is nothing but positive," the reporter says.

Funny I've been told the opposite. I was informed by the producers, on many occasions, that people tolerated me. I didn't look like someone who should win, so we shouldn't be surprised if we didn't win.

"You have to be kidding. Are you sure they are talking about me?"

"Yes. Here are some of them." He passes me the papers, and I read a few. He's right. Why did I believe the producers?

"Thank you for showing me these. I needed this to keep me going."

Mitch kindly excuses himself and doesn't return for the next part of the interview. He didn't attend school here so he would have no idea what is going on in town. Conner joins me and together we walk the halls of the school. We explore the school and I try to remember the good times. We walk past to my old locker, the choir room and the school library. This place looks nothing like I remember. We turn down the hallway toward the auditorium and I continue to point out the highlights and low moments of my school career. The new drama teacher must've been able to find some old videos of performances I did in the archives. He turns them over to be added in the video package.

I gape at Conner, my mouth wide open, when he admits he used to sneak into the auditorium and watch me rehearse whatever show or concert I was working on. He told vivid details about my audition for the senior musical.

I can't believe it. He really did care back then even though I never would've believed it. I thought the idea of me being his little secret was a fetish of his. I see him differently for the first time since that awful day over ten years ago. I can't help it, I love him. To know he used to find ways to be close to me without my or anyone else's knowledge, makes me feel special and cherished.

Our time at the school concludes and I'm ready to get back to the studio. This is bittersweet for me. I want to be angry and shout back to the defenseless building, give it the middle finger. So much pain existed here once, but now I realize the hurt placed me on this path to where I am now, and I wouldn't change it for the world.

The SUV pulls up to the airport and I'm ready to leave.

Boarding the plane, a sense of peace washes over me. I'm ready to finish this competition and for the first time, I want to finish on top.

Our schedule is timed out to the second and has us returning to the studio just in time for dress rehearsal. I am a tightly wound ball of nerves during rehearsal.

Despite the encouraging letters I read today, and the progress I've made so far, I still wonder if I'm ready. I will always have the doubts in my head telling me the opposite. I need to fight this feeling with the new-found confidence I found.

We fly through dress rehearsal without much of an issue. The live show is starting in an hour, and my anxiety is at an all-time high. Something feels off. I keep checking my clothes and hair. I look online to see what is being posted. Nothing. Chalk it up to pre-show jitters, I suppose.

After a short hour of waiting on last minute finalizations and watching the ticket-holders file into their seats, the music blasts over the speakers as my cue to bring in the beginning of the episode.

I enter from stage left, holding my mic like I have been instructed. I'm singing while I saunter to my mark on the center of the platform. The spectators cheer, nearly drowning out the song.

Terri moves in from the other side of the stage and meets me in the middle, giving me an encouraging wink. She chimes in, harmonizing with the chorus then belts out her own stanza.

It is one of the most surreal moments of my life.

The song ends, and she hugs me. I hold my hands out toward Terri and announce, "Terri Nunn, everyone." The audience hops up in a wave of screaming, clapping, smiling faces.

The judges stand with the crowd, offering praise and commending me on how far I've come in my journey. It is a lovefest.

When they break for commercial, I run into the dressing room and change for song two. I slip into the 1950's red and white polka-dot chiffon dress, feeling very sexy. The hair-dresser rolls my hair and pins the curls into place off my face while the make-up artist tones down my make-up and applies cherry-red lipstick to my lips. I look like a pinup girl, especially in the shiny bright-red heels I'm rocking.

I walk out of the dressing room, my head held high, and notice Mitch stop dead in his tracks in the doorway to his room. He stares at me, his mouth wide open. His skin flushes, and his pupils dilate.

I play down the lust in his eyes, and wave, "You might want to close your mouth. You are letting the flies in." I tease as I stare back at him with an unsure smile. What is wrong with him? He hasn't looked at me like that since before our break up.

He closes his mouth and clears his throat before, leading me to the wings where the stage manager hands me a mic and Mitch his guitar. "You ready?" I hear a voice ask over the monitors in my ears. Like every week before, the video package of the past events leading up to tonight is shown. The hometown visit, the concert, the interview, everything that was shot, but it is edited much better this time around. Even our emotional interviews going into this duet are more uplifting.

I bounce on my toes, too excited to hold it in. This is my night to turn into the butterfly I always knew I could be, to finally shed the last of my chrysalis of negativity and fly.

We are introduced, and I place my mic on the stand. The unearthed energy flows as Mitch starts the first stanza. He gives me a side glance while he sings the first line. I join in on the next phrase of the duet and turn my body toward him as acting the part takes hold. We peer at each other singing about romance and taking chances. I prance closer to Mitch, smoothing my hand over his shoulder and resting my head on his upper arm, finding the familiarity of our past relationship as a couple.

When I glance up, he's looking at me with a passion in his eyes that is far more genuine than what I'm feeling. My mind goes into panic mode while continuing the facade on the stage. I back away from him casually, trying to recoil from some unseen boundary I may have crossed without knowing. He chases me, determined to keep our connection.

I keep wondering what would Conner be thinking if he was here right now.

The song ends, and before I can retract, he dives in, kissing me. I glare at him and mouth, "What the fuck are you doing?" He smirks and leans in for another kiss. I jerk back and bitch-slap him. My mind runs over what I did to entice him to kiss me, not only once but twice. In a panic, I search the audience. My suspicions are correct, Conner stands out against the shocked crowd, red-faced and wringing his hands. Anger radiates off him like steam off boiling water.

I'm too stunned by Mitch and to upset over Conner to leave the stage. The host hurries out to us, fumbling with his words, likely as stunned as I am. "We'll be right back after this," he blurts. Someone calls "cut" and "five minutes, people" in the distance.

Once we are off the stage, I push Mitch. He huffs out a surprised breath and raises his brows. "What was that for?"

"What are you trying to do?" I see fear in his eyes. He knows he did something wrong. "Conner and I are together. Conner is here, you idiot, and saw the whole thing." I gesture to the audience. "Do you have a death wish?" I catch Conner walking through the exit from the corner of my eye.

Tears burn my eyes. My breathing spikes to a pace I can't control. I can't lose him over this. It isn't even my fault. Panic consumes me. My chest tightens. I just want to curl into a ball on the floor and pretend this never happened. If only I can be transported back in time and change this incident I would.

Chapter 34

Serena

After a minute that seems to drag on forever, I find my footing in reality again and pull myself out of a full-on anxiety attack. I look up at Mitch, grinding my teeth, my face twisted in a sneer. I shove past him and ram him into the wall with my shoulder.

Determined to fix this, I make my way out of the building. I hear Mitch call in the distance, "I'm sorry. The producers thought it would be a great idea to drum up votes."

I turn around. What did he just say?

Mitch continues. "They wanted to create a love triangle in the press and on the show to gain more viewers. They said it would help us in the voting, and I agreed to it because I think we can win this."

"If this is how we win, then I don't want any part of it. Either you fix this, or I am out!" I turn around and walk out the door.

Thank goodness, a car was waiting. The only thing I can think of is getting to Conner and making things right. The car ride takes forever. I could've crossed the Red Sea in the amount of time it takes to get to the hotel.

I race to his room before he tries to run away from me and all this crazy. My heart drops with dread.

There was no mistaking his tense muscles and red face for anything other than fury when he left the studio.

Conner's door is ajar and I open it without knocking. His suitcase is out, and he is throwing clothes in. The sharp angles of his features tighten with each curse he mumbles under his breath.

My throat tightens around a lump of desperate emotion. He is leaving. How could he believe I would want Mitch over him?

I slam the door behind me and let my purse fall to the floor at my feet. Conner's back stiffens, and he spins toward me, pinning me under his angry gaze. His misperceived notions and ire are dragging him away from me.

"How long? How long have you two been together?" He asks through gritted teeth.

I rush around the bed, surrendering to him. "Nothing is going on between me and Mitch, I swear. What you saw was a game the producers were playing to get ratings. I am at my whit's end over this. If you want me to leave the competition, I will. I never want you to think I would be unfaithful."

Not paying attention to my words he continues shouting. "I guess you want him more. He accepted you without prejudice. He wasn't afraid," he runs his fingers through his hair in frustration. "I was the one who couldn't bring my love for you to the fore front. I had to be judgmental like the rest of them. To be one of them!"

I shake my head and match his volume. Time to dredge this up yet again. Let this please be the last time so we can put this to bed. If we can't this will be the never-ending vicious cycle always coming between us. "Why was being one of them so important? I never understood why you couldn't be the way you wanted. The person I saw that no one else got to see." I start to pace. My heart is racing and I need to get this out now. "You were a walking contradiction. I honestly never knew which was the real you. The Dr. Jekyll and Mr. Hyde act messed me up. Every time we were together, I would think you'd come clean, accept me for who I was and make me feel like I was important to you—"

Conner grabs me mid-step and stops my pacing. "Don't you understand? You were important— are important— to me. I didn't know how to blend the two. I wish I could change things, but I can't. My parents believed that we had to keep up appearances, and that meant the girls I dated had to look and act a certain way. Why, I have no clue. I was tired of how they wanted me to behave as opposed to how I wanted to be. How I wanted to exist. To make the choices I wanted to. My choice would have been you. Always you."

"Are you saying I was your act of rebellion? Let's stick it to mom and dad and date the fat girl. Oh wait, you couldn't stick it to them because you were afraid of public opinion. Get a clue, Conner. I was a human being with feelings and you played with them in some sick game. How do I know you want me now because of me, not my success and appearance? Or is it because your parents finally approve of me?" I cross my arms and huff. "I am aware it always comes back to this." I couldn't take it anymore, and I raise my hands. "How do we get past this? Where do we go from here?"

I feel like the room is spinning and the air escaped from the atmosphere. The dam broke, and inconsolable sobs racked my body.

As I am sinking to the ground, I feel two strong arms grab me around my waist and steady me to the floor. His hand cups my cheek and urges my head to lay against his chest. He murmurs, "Shh now. Everything will be fine." Between my hiccupping cries, I hear, "I love you." His fingers gently remove the pins holding back my hair so his hands can sift through it. I look up at eyes just as swollen and forlorn as mine must look.

"Remember the time I came to your house? I snuck in and scared you. You were in your own little world. I watched you for a good five minutes before I even said a word. I remember this girl singing at the top of her lungs some Broadway showtune. You looked so happy and so sure of yourself, and you matched the singer on the CD note for note." He kisses my hair. "All I ever wanted was to be like you in that moment. Free. It's the same way I look at you now. And when I see someone else skirt on your effortless kindness, it makes me angry. You are mine, I am yours, and I need other men, like Mitch, to respectfully back off. They need to understand we will not be separated."

My tears dry. He leans in, giving me a kiss laced with promise and love.

Chapter 35

Serena

Two weeks have passed, and it's finale time. We survived controversy and eliminations to get to the final 2. I can't believe we've come so far. My face hurts from the huge grin I'm sporting, and butterflies are constantly bouncing around in my belly. Vindication is mine. I've waited for this moment for so long. No matter what happens, I'll be happy knowing we gave it our best and got to live out a once in a lifetime experience.

Deciding which song to pick from the approved list for this week is much harder than the past weeks. I want something that speaks of the positivity of this day, but I am too afraid of choosing the wrong one. I look over the options, biting my lip in uncertainty, then hold the paper out to Mitch. "You do it," I tell him.

"I think we need to choose this song." He points to the song-title on the paper.

My eyes grow wide at the suggestion. The power of his choice surges through me.

"You know... Let's take it full circle. I know this song means a lot to you."

Considering Mitch's suggestion, I feel a wave of emotion roll over me. I tug at the hem of my shirt. I feel like I'm sixteen and at Sally's birthday party again. "I agree. Let's get to work."

We go over the song line by line, phrase by phrase, note by painstaking note, for what seems like days. The time seems to be dragging on, and I want this over and finished so I can move on to the next step. Whether it's a celebration or a quiet cry in the corner, I don't care. I just want some time to be with Conner. He continues to be my rock, giving me compliments and building my self-esteem in any way he can.

Conner is trying to work past this hiccup. Mitch is making an attempt to bridge a friendship. Conner listened to Mitch and is attempting to accept a move to friendship. Either way, they will both be in my life. This duo will continue after the cameras have turned away and all we have left is our music.

The next few days fly by in a whirlwind of interviews, rehearsals, and recordings. Just as I'm finding my confidence and think I have the show in the bag, I come across a copy of the latest rag. The blurb features me with a crappy picture, making me look like a big, ugly blob.

I am through with this. Tears cool the angry heat radiating from my face. I'm done overlooking the constant judgement by the show and slander in the magazines. I roll up the piece of trash and twist, crumpling the magazine in my fists until the pages tear. I've dealt with this crap long enough. I am so done with this. Just because I don't look like the average stick on TV, they are quick to ridicule. I decide it is time to take no prisoners.

"Welcome to the season finale of 'Next Vocal Thing.' We have the remaining contestants ready for the final challenge."

To excite the crowd, the lights come alive with strobes of color and the opening of "the final countdown" begins.

This is it. Our moment. Mitch and I have worked our asses off to get here. We walk down the stairs toward the host. Smiling for the camera is becoming second nature to me. Mitch holds my hand and reassures me. His touch reminds me that I'm not alone, and I relax.

I scan the crowd and find my family first. They are all holding signs and cheering me on. I glance at Mitch as he waves to his family. I don't see Conner anywhere in the audience. Last we spoke, he said he was going to be here. He assured me.

Disappointment starts to settle in my heart. Accepting that Conner didn't show, I return my gaze to the host.

"I love you, Serena," echoes over the hushed crowd. Conner skips down the steps, finding his seat in a rush as he smiles and waves to me. My fake smile turns genuine. My Conner. He came. Just like he promised.

Chapter 36

Conner

I didn't think I was going to make it. My plane was late, then the cab hit a traffic jam, and all I could think about was getting there.

I make a beeline to my seat just in time to hear the host announce my girl's name. I watch her with pride. This is it. Serena is going to win. She has too.

They go to commercial, and Mitch and Serena adjust their mics. Hair and makeup arrive, fluffing her curls while dabbing at her face. She looks beautiful. She always does just like she always did.

I look across the aisle and spot Serena's parents. Mr. and Mrs. Ashby soak in all the behind-the-scenes movement with large, adoring eyes. Mrs. Ashby is holding a big poster sign that reads, 'WE LOVE YOU, MITCH AND SERENA."

My smile falters, realizing how much groveling I'll need to do to gain their trust. All they see is their little girl heartbroken in a hospital.

I hear in the distance a guy shout, "Marry Me Serena!" I see the signs everywhere too. I know they are there every week, but that's my woman on the stage. She belongs to me and I plan to make it official as soon as I think she is ready. I know it's too soon but we are meant to be.

I train my attention back on Serena. The stage is hers. She commands the audience with such vigor. Their hunger for her stirs a bit of jealousy in my gut. I love her and, yes I want the fans to love her too, but deep down, I want her all to myself. Every minute of every day, she consumes my thoughts and dreams.

"The wheel..." She breaks into song, and I smile, a warmth spreading from my heart to the rest of my body. This song means everything to her. The idea that life can circle back again is her mantra. Her favorite line comes through the microphone. "The truth moves through us even when we sleep."

I gulp down a lump of emotion. I need to hold it in and be strong. She is amazing, and she is all mine.

Standing before the cameras, she waves and makes the phone sign. She needs the votes.

I love her no matter what she looks like or what she does. To me, she will always be that girl at the party, in the closet. I knew then, my life would change, no matter how much I fought it.

Chapter 37

Serena

I strut like a peacock and become one with the music. I gaze into the audience and sing only to Conner. This song is my everything. My life's lesson.

The truth is... I am terrified. We could win this show, and even though at this moment I can guarantee our lives are going to change, winning will take it to a whole new level.

I belt out the final chorus as if my life depends on it. Mitch matches my intensity with his guitar, wailing out the last few notes and letting them fade into a beautiful hum.

We have come so far. I never thought I would be able to work with him. I am so glad I did. Our past has made this awkward relationship into a powerful and profitable friendship.

I end the song in an empowering pose and smile. We face the judges. "Serena, I don't know where your spirit comes from. You are in it to win it. Congratulations!" Doesn't matter what happens now. We are stars. This isn't the end win or lose.

"Yeah, I agree, you and Mitch are just amazing. Great song choice. You made the song your own. You are the ones to beat."

"I will keep on the Serena and Mitch bandwagon." Brett Thompson rises up and shouts.

Triumph continues with the words of praise. "You're on fire!"

"You guys are HOT!" I beam from ear-to-ear hearing Sylvia words.

Grayson Twist turns to camera two. "Thank you to the judges. Ok, audience, the ball is in your court. To vote for Serena and Mitch, dial 888-555-4848. Now, after the break, the other group still in contention, Crew Shull Timing, will be hitting the stage for your votes."

I hear a voice overhead saying, "We're out. Back in five."

The host takes us aside. "I know you want to win this. If you don't, I wouldn't worry. As a matter of fact, I am starting a record label with one of the judges, and we would like you on our roster of artists."

Doubt creeps over my glow of confidence. What if we didn't win, and this idea is just a setup? "That is awfully generous of you, but my contract states I can't make any decisions while I am a part of this show. Let's wait and see what the outcome is first before we discuss this any further."

Crew Shull Timing take the stage. The cheering couldn't have been louder. They are clearly the viewers' favorite. The press loves them. They have the teen girl, middle aged women and gay males' fingers on mandatory redial. Skippy is the favorite of the foursome. His perfect hair and bright blue eyes capture everyone's attention. Classic boy band material. His smooth moves charm them all.

Once the performance is finished, they move to the center of the stage. Their brilliant smiles and tense bodies display their desire to win.

I don't know what I want more, to win and get the whole packaged deal that comes with the show, or lose and choose my path. Fate lies in the results.

Mitch and I gather, shoulder to shoulder, with the members of Crew while we wait for the votes to tally up. The host announces, "We will have the results after this message." We cut to commercial.

My heartbeat pounds in my chest and thumps in my ears, drowning out the audience's chatter. Show members speak to me as they fiddle with our mics and make-up, but all I hear is wha-wha-wha. Don't they understand I'm hanging off a cliff waiting on the answer? I want it now. My future depends on the little envelope being handed to the host.

"We're back, and the results are in. The winner of this season's Next Big Thing is…."

I draw in a deep breath and grab Mitch's hand.

"The winner is Crew Shull Timing."

Chapter 38

Serena

Confetti blasts toward the crowd, and the roar of cheering raised to a high decibel.

I stand stick-still in shock. Even though I said I would be okay if we didn't win, I was still hoping for it.

I look at Mitch and smile. I then peer over the crowd to Conner and my parents and give a smirk with a wave. Forcing back the waterworks, I offer the cameras and the winners my best "pageant" smile.

The cameras are still rolling. I wave at the audience as if I'm not disappointed. The stage exit is calling my name, and I walk off. It's okay that we didn't win. I realize it's not the end of my career, but the beginning.

The past few months have been chaotic to say the least. Between interviews, touring and songwriting, I stay exhausted, but in a good way. The monotonous days on the bus are starting to wear me down. It is stifling my creative flow. I miss Conner, and no amount of phone calls or text messages compensate for his touch, for him to be in the flesh holding me. I am really looking forward to the break from the road.

We'll get into the studio in two months and start recording. The record contract comes quickly, and they say we're going to make the music we want.

Ballroom Blitz has already asked if we can perform on the show. I request that Ivan be involved with the choreography and performance. I know if he is featured, he may have an opportunity to get out from the troupe and dance with the actual stars.

The mile markers keep changing. Another city, another performance awaiting us. The calendar in my hand tells the tale of my journey. My handwriting scribbles out notes of where I've been and where I'm going.

My phone buzzes with an awaiting message.

Conner: Miss you. When will I see you? It's driving me crazy, but I can wait while you go and become a rock star.
Me: How is tomorrow? We are on our way back now. Two days off before we leave again.

I look around the cramped quarters with pride and amazement. How did I get here? Patience in waiting my turn at the big prize? I'm flying high. Yes! I won the jackpot. To think I almost didn't have this. I waited for the other half of my soul for so long. To think I almost didn't let him back in out of fear. Conner makes me feel confident and beautiful.

Laying in my bunk on the bus, I stare at a picture we took last month. We were looking into each other eyes. His expression says it all. The love we have is real, and I want more than anything to keep it forever. To keep him forever.

My phone dings again.

Conner: Get some sleep, love. You will need it. I plan to keep you up all night. ;)

I shiver with excitement. He knows how to get my fire started. It's getting rather warm in here.

Me: I can't wait. Love you.

After a few hours of shut-eye, I hop out of my bunk and shuffle over to the coffee-maker. The wafting smell of java permeates the space. I retrieve my favorite mug from the small cupboard above my head. I slide into the empty booth with my pen and pad in hand, settling into the relaxing rock of the bus. Finally, I get a speck of inspiration through my haze of fatigue. Who knew, I'd get the urge to write with so much distraction in my life right now.

Mitch approaches from the back of the bus. After some counseling, we were able to really put this partnership in a great place. There's a sense of trust between us again.

After all the comments, arguments and foolish childhood behavior, Conner trusts Mitch on the road with me. He finally knows we are more like brother and sister than former lovers.

I'm furiously writing down the words while humming and don't see Mitch slid into the seat across from me. He taps a finger against my paper. "So, what are you writing?"

His voice stirs me from deep, creative thinking. "Take a gander." I pass the notepad across the laminated table surface. There are scribbles everywhere.

Looking at me with surprise, he starts to laugh. "How do you make something out of this chaos?"

"I will clean it up once I finish my train of thought." I place pen to paper and continue.

He rises from his seat and heads toward the back. "Serena, I'm so glad everything seems to be working out for you. And for me too."

"You know what? I agree. I am finally happy with who I am and who I am with. Who knew it would take this journey to get me here? Everything happens for a reason."

"It certainly does." Mitch closes the door to the back room behind him.

Gazing out of the tinted window, I watch the dark blur of trees and road zoom by. I inhale a deep breath and sigh.

It certainly does. It certainly does!

Epilogue

Serena

1 year later

I set the pen down on the notepad and close the book. I can't believe it. I have another song in the books. I hope Mitch is good with this one. Just as I am putting my journal away, the computer chimes. I will never get used to the luxury of having Wi-Fi on a tour bus. I click on the screen and Conner appears. "Hey there, what are you up to? This isn't our normal time to Skype?"

He is looking at me with the big grin I truly adore. The corners of my mouth quirk up automatically in response. "I got out early. Where are you performing tonight?"

"Chicago. I am so tired. All I want to do is get in my room, order room service, shower and crawl into bed. I'm beat." I glance behind him, and it looks like he is chatting with me from a coffee house. "Where are you?"

"Out in town. They opened a new coffee shop."

I know something is up because his cheeks are turning pink.

"I should be back in town for two nights before we leave for the road again. Keep the bed warm, and I will be there soon enough."

I lug my bags through the door of my hotel room and drop them just inside. The sweet smell of flowers fills my nose, and my eyes land on a bright bouquet of roses and baby's breath.

Stopping in front of the mirror next to the desk, I examine the miles of wear and tear on my features. I may not be the size of a supermodel, but I am me. As Oprah says, "my true, authentic self."

I move toward the flowers and flip up the card dangling around the vase to read it. I smile. It's from Conner.

My heart is never far from yours.
Conner

My eyes well up with tears. Isn't life good? I have my dream career, my first love, and all without sacrificing who I am at my core.

There's a knock on the door just as my phone rings. I snatch my cell from my purse, answering Mitch's call, and approach the door. "Mitch, can you give me a minute?" I swing open the door to find Conner grinning wide. I shrill. I place my hand over my mouth. "What are you doing here?"

"I arranged with Mitch and your assistant, Jess, to clear your schedule for me today. So, there are no interviews, no personal appearances, just you and me for the whole day." He flicks his finger over my nose. "There is somewhere I want to take you."

I am extremely curious. My jacket is thrown over the chair near the door. I accept his hand and pluck my jacket off the chair on the way out. I feel the jerk on my arm and a belly laugh from Conner dragging me down the hallway.

We leave the hotel and grab a taxi. I overhear Conner tell the driver to take us to the bean.

Ten minutes later, the cab drops us off at a street corner, and Conner pulls me along behind him. We follow the walkway to a reflective, silver bean sculpture. Puffs of our breath swirl into the cold air, and I tug my coat a little closer. Conner pulls me toward him so we are facing each other. The warmth of love and contentment heats my shivering body. I enjoy moments like these. They are far and few between.

"Serena, we have been through hell and back. Hell, that I wrongfully placed on you. You gave me the second and third chance that I didn't deserve. I owe everything to you. To our life."

Conner swirls me back around so my back is facing his front. I look at our reflection, and he's snuggling me closer. We fit perfectly together. He kisses my neck and I see stars. Breaking his hold, I twist back. This is the best day ever. I gaze into his eyes, and I can see the love I feel echoed in their depths.

He holds up his finger gesturing I give him a minute, then lowers to the cold ground on one knee. Passers-by take notice and gather around us, pointing their phones. This will end up on TMZ, for sure.

He continues, "You showed me strength and love when I didn't deserve it. Serena, I want to take the next step with you. I want to wake up knowing you are really, truly mine. I love you and want to spend my life with you. Serena, my love, will you marry me?"

I have dreamt about this day over and over again. "This is all I ever wanted. I've wanted this since I was seventeen and you kissed me in the closet. Of course, I will marry you. It's you and me until the end."

He jumps up, expelling a sigh of relief, and jerks me to his chest. Dipping me back in his arms, he kisses me. Once he gives me a thorough show of his affection, he tips me upright and spins around to the crowd, shouting, "She said yes. She said yes."

I giggle as he fists bumps the air, realizing that I am worthy of this life, one filled with self-respect, a man who worships me, and a future that will lead me to my dreams.

THE END

Acknowledgements

First and foremost, I need to thank my readers. Thank you for starting this crazy journey with me.

Ari and Hannah thank you for believing in me and allowing me the time to work on this. Mommy loves you!

To Dad who pushed me to finish. I wouldn't be here without you.

To my beautiful Mom who was brutally honest and told me to finish this story. I'm sorry you weren't here to see the finished product but I know you are cheering me on from the great beyond.

To Aunt Carol, Aunt Ros, Jennifer, and Rebecca: Thank you for being there when I needed you.

To all my family. If it wasn't for your love and patience, I wouldn't be here.

To Haven Cage for my awesome book design and talking me off the ledge.

To Jeni for your amazing edits. The book wouldn't be this incredible without your help.

To Nicole, Haven, Carrie, Heidi, April, Laura, Renee, Annie, Jill, LK, Julie, Melissa, Amy, Jen, Whitney, Kristi, Shalia and Sophia for hearing me and holding my hand as I drove you insane.

To my first beta readers who weren't afraid to be honest and gave constructive criticism.

To the Window Lockers for taking the time on a new author.

To the past who helped me understand who I was.

Biography

Just a Long Island girl living in a Southern world….

20 years ago, a Jew moved from the comfort of her Long Island home for parts unknown of South Carolina. She had to learn and adapt to the ways of the South, real quick like. For years, she was on a quest for Northern goodies in a Southern town. However, the journey for the proper bagel and the perfect NYC pizza always eluded her. The ever-loving theater geek craved the bright lights of the big city and planned to return someday.

All her plans changed when she attempted to settle down and marry. Five years later, she found herself the mother of "life experiment #1", a boy. Then exactly five years afterward, "life experiment #2," a girl came along. Both are every bit as eclectic as she is. Boy Experiment sings The Beastie Boys and Taylor Swift on demand, while Girl Experiment shouts "Where is Thumpkin" with the gusto of a head-banging Metal God all while wearing her Wonder Woman nightgown.

Adding to the family fun is Bronco the beagle, a rescue that has not only given them hours of entertainment but so much love too.

Sometimes God listens to your plans and laughs at them, and with Sarah, this has been no exception. From surviving a divorce, losing her mother to a short battle with the C-word, and learning to navigate through life with her widowed Vietnam Veteran father and her amazingly resilient kids, times have changed.

Over the years, she's adapted, making a life with her B.A. in Theatre Performance in hand. She continues to find balance between Faith and the delights of slower Southern living. Though she misses the hustle and bustle of the Big Apple, Sarah is now fluent in "Bless your hearts" and understanding the importance of pearl-clutching. Her family humors her and enjoys her antics. That's all she needs, no matter her geographical location.

If you're interested in learning more about Sarah and her books, you can reach out to her at authorslroth@gmail.com, or you can follow her at any of these links:

- Facebook
- Instagram
- Bookbub
- Goodreads
- Amazon Author Page
- SarahLRothauthor.com

Want to stay up to date on all of Sarah's upcoming news, books, and events? Sign up for her newsletter at https://sendfox.com/authorslroth

Don't forget to check out Sarah's holiday short story, The Dreidel Spin on Amazon!